A RUTHLESS CHRISTMAS

RUTHLESS KINGS MC: BOOK NINE

K.L. SAVAGE

COPYRIGHT© 2020 A RUTHLESS CHRISTMAS BY KL SAVAGE

All rights reserved. Except as permitted by U.S. Copyright Act of 1976, no part of this publication may be reproduced, distributed, or transmitted in any form or by any means, or stored in a database or retrieval system, without prior permission of the author. The scanning, uploading, and distribution of this book via the Internet or via other means without the permission of the publisher is illegal and punishable by law. Please purchase only authorized electronic editions and do not participate in or encourage electronic piracy of copyrighted materials. This book is a work of fiction. Names, characters, establishments, or organizations, and incidents are either products of the author's imagination or are used fictitiously to give a sense of authenticity. Any resemblance to actual persons, living or dead, events, or locales is entirely coincidental. A RUTHLESS CHIRSTMAS is intended for 18+ older, and for mature audiences only.

ISBN: 979-8-578092-96-1
LCCN 9781952500268

PHOTOGRAPHY BY WANDER AGUIAR PHOTOGRAPHY
COVER MODEL: SONNY & JOLI
EBOOK COVER DESIGN: WANDER AGUIAR
EDITING: MASQUE OF THE RED PEN & INFINITE WELL
FORMATTING: CHAMPAGNE BOOK DESIGN

FIRST EDITION PRINT 2020

For everyone who believes in Christmas miracles.
We hope we find yours this holiday season.

CHAPTER ONE

Reaper

One week until Christmas, and I haven't done any shopping, of any sorts, for anyone. That includes Sarah. I'm fucked. Santa is going to put fucking coals under the tree for me and burn my damn stocking. Who the hell waits this long? I don't know what to get her. I'm stressed the hell out.

Which means I'm hiding outside around back of the clubhouse because I need a damn smoke.

The damn Christmas carols, the jingle bells, the fucking Christmas movies; I'm about to drown in snow. And guess what?

It doesn't fucking snow in Vegas!

Well, it hasn't since I was a kid, but knowing my luck, this will be the year we get a record blizzard. And I can hear everyone now, "Let's go sledding! Let's make snow angels; let's build a snowman!"

Fucking shoot me.

But before any of that, I need a gift for Sarah, or so help me I'll never see another Christmas again.

I rub my temples, exhaling the stress of the holidays in a puff of air that clouds out in front of me because it's cold.

I hate being cold. I miss the heat. I miss the sun making me sweat and my skin turning pink.

I'm a damn scrooge.

Ho-ho-freaking-ho.

The pack of cigarettes in my cut pocket weigh against my right pec. I open the delicate leather and bury my hand inside, yanking the pack out. I pound the end of the box against my palm so I can tighten that tobacco. I take my time opening the container. Something about this moment is going to feel so fucking good, and I want to relish it. My fingers slide against the sleek, smooth stick. I glide out the cigarette and bring it to my nose, inhaling the rich, earthy scent.

"Oh god," I moan. It's been so long since I've had a smoke. I can't wait a second longer. I put the orange end between my lips, strike the lighter, cup my hand over the tip, and inhale. Ash starts to form, turning a beautiful shade of crimson. The smoke trickles down my throat, spreading over my lungs in the most toxic way.

I love it.

"Don't let Sarah see, or she'll think you're cheating," Poodle says as he comes around the corner of the clubhouse.

Taking another long drag, I blow the smoke in his face, not laughing at his joke. It isn't funny. I'd never fuck around on my doll. "Don't speak that way to me," I say, flicking the ashes from the tip. "I'm a little stressed. I needed a break from—"

"Christmas?"

"Christmas," I say on a tired sigh.

"We're supposed to go get a tree tonight. We've waited long enough. The kids are getting antsy."

"I'm not going."

"Are you pouting? Is Prez really throwing a tantrum?"

"Say that to me again and see what happens."

"Jesse!"

"Fuck, fuck, fuck." I throw the cigarette down and stomp on it. Poodle waves his arms through the air to get rid of the smoke. "Get rid of it!" I blow the rest out of my mouth, then start spitting. "Sarah's going to kill me."

"I'm trying to get rid of it," Poodle hisses. "It isn't my fault you're a damn chimney!"

"Do not make Santa Clause jokes right now," I snap in return, rubbing my tongue on my shirt sleeve to get the smoke out of my mouth.

"Oh, yeah. Real smooth Reaper. That's going to work. You need a freaking blow torch to get rid of the stench wafting off you."

"What's going on, guys?" Sarah's sweet voice comes from the left.

Poodle and I casually lean against the siding, pretending to talk about Christmas. "Hey, Doll. Don't come any further!" I stop her when she takes a step forward.

Her face falls when she sees she isn't welcome. "Why not? Maizey is asleep, Home Alone isn't on, and I thought we could—"

"Doll, I'm talking about your Christmas gifts. You can't know."

Her face brightens more than the damn sun when she hears the word 'gifts.' My Doll deserves all the gifts in the world.

If only I could figure out what the hell to get her.

"Really?" She rocks on her heels, cupping her hands in front of her. "What kind of gifts?"

I smirk, feeling like a real asshole for lying to her, but I don't want to tell her I've been smoking. I don't think she'll be too upset. She isn't controlling, but she's worried for my health. I only have one or two cigarettes a week, which is less than what I used to smoke.

"I can't tell you that, Doll. It would ruin the surprise. Now, let me brainstorm with Poodle. I'll catch you and Maizey in a few. Later, we'll go get that tree you want so bad."

"The biggest one they have?"

"Doll, I know how much you love big things," I purr, lowering my voice so she can't miss the sexual innuendo.

She blushes, looks over at Poodle, who is currently laughing, and then slides her eyes back to me. "Jesse, we aren't alone."

I love how bashful she gets sometimes.

"I know."

"Do I need to leave?" Poodle asks, pointing back and forth between me and Sarah. "Maybe give you a little privacy?"

I'm about to tell him to get out of fucking dodge when something bites my ankle. I immediately stumble away and hop on one foot in pain. "Ow, what the f—"

I look around to find the culprit, but it's dark. Then I hear a low hiss come from out of the darkness. "Son of a bitch! What was that?"

"Happy! Where'd you go?" Tongue yells out his pet gator's name.

I meet the eyes of my nemesis on the ground, its mouth wide open and baring its little fangs. He's still hissing at me. The damned thing swishes its tail, charges at me, and I do the only thing that enters my mind.

I hiss back.

"Oh my god!" Poodle falls over chuckling, and so does Sarah. Both of them are gripping their stomachs while I limp from a damn gator bite.

"This is not funny!" I snap. The wound isn't that bad. Tiny dots of blood, but that's not the point. That fucking gator is feral. "Tongue! Get your damn … kitten." I can't believe he calls it that, but whatever makes Tongue mellow and grounded, then so be it.

Tongue comes around the corner and puts his hands on his thighs, relieved that he found his pet. "Oh, thank goodness. Maizey said she forgot to close the top to the tank; I was worried he would have gotten too far."

"Don't worry about him attacking people or anything." I roll my eyes, hobbling on one foot.

"He didn't attack you." Tongue rolls his eyes and claps his hands together. "Come here, Happy."

The little shit has the nerve to hiss at me again as he scurries over to Tongue, clicking up small clouds of dust with his paws. The talons click along the pebbles, and when I narrow my eyes, I notice something different about Happy's nails. They are painted red.

Is this some type of joke?

Poodle sees what I'm staring at and leans over to inspect the claws. "That's a nice shade," he observes.

"You like it? I picked it out. It reminded me of blood."

"No kidding?" Poodle says, clearly not surprised, but pretending to be. "I wouldn't have guessed, Tongue."

I bring the attention back to me. "Do you see the tear in my jeans?" I ask, turning to the left and kicking my leg out so he can see the gaping freaking hole. "He bit me."

Tongue bends over and picks up Happy, cradling him in one arm like a baby and starts tickling its belly. "It was a love bite. He didn't mean no harm, Prez."

"A love…" I say on a small breath that falls out of me when I hear such a thing. "A love bite? You cannot be serious. You better keep a freaking leash on him, Tongue. I won't have him hurting the kids."

"He loves the kids! Everyone's seen it. He loves playing fetch with Maizey."

"You're saying your gator doesn't like me? Is that it?" I ask, moving my eyes to Poodle who's whistling and staring at the sky as if it has painted him a pretty picture.

Sarah is filming the interaction on her phone, and I know I'm never going to live this down.

"Well, Prez … yeah, you need to earn his trust. You're the only one who pays him no mind."

"Tongue, I pay him no mind because he bites me!" I shout, then lower my voice when exhaustion hits. "All I wanted was two minutes of alone time. Two. Then, I get eaten by a damn gator," I start mumbling under my breath as I limp away. "All I wanted was a smoke. All I wanted was to figure out what

A RUTHLESS CHRISTMAS

to get Sarah." I make sure no one can hear what I'm saying except me.

"Where are you going, Prez?" Poodle calls out to me.

"Away from that damn thing!" I wave my arm back, hoping Happy gets the damn point.

"Reaper!" Sarah saying my road name has me stopping in my tracks. A droplet of blood runs down my leg when I put my weight on it. A small bead of blood, but I've killed for less, and I can't fucking kill a family pet. That's beneath me. "Give me your pack of cigarettes, right now."

Damn it. I was just about to go find a hiding spot to have a smoke. "Doll, just one," I beg. I flash her the biggest smile I can muster, but she holds her palm out and gestures her fingers for me to give up the goods.

I hate Christmas.

And Happy can go back to the damn swamp for all I care. Bah-fucking-humbug.

CHAPTER TWO

Sarah

REAPER HAS BEEN SO CRANKY LATELY. I KNOW EVERYTHING has been tense. There's still a lingering tension between me and Tongue, and Tongue and Reaper. Tongue accidentally stabbed me, thinking I was his uncle. He was upset, his mind racing as he went back in time to when his uncle did unspeakable things to him. The other members found his journals, journals I didn't even know about, and they looked through them without his permission.

Tongue broke.

He was only fighting for himself, and I don't blame him for that.

But we got into a fight. He said things, I said things, and now we don't say anything to each other.

I miss my best friend. Not that he needs me anymore; he has Daphne. Who is beyond perfect for him and so damn sweet that I don't even know how they work? No, that's not true. Tongue is sweet, kind, and fragile. No one would know that they have to handle him with ease because he's big, bad, and scary.

He's happy, and I miss him. I want to know how he's doing, but I'm too nervous to confront him. Our pride is getting in the way of making amends, and I don't know how to lower the wall that's been built between us.

All I can do is hope when the right time comes, everything will resolve itself.

Like my wound. It was deep, but it healed quicker than Doc thought, and now I'm back on my feet. I got cleared for sex weeks ago.

And I'm going to make Reaper's day and make him happier than a damn clam. I open the baby pink box I got downtown from the lingerie shop Juliette used to work at and grin when I see a handwritten note from Trixie.

"Go get'em, tiger."

Gosh, she's such a hoot. She doesn't hang around much; actually, she doesn't at all, and I don't understand why. Reaper says Trixie finds it too painful to be around the club because her brother Hawk died. Sometimes I forget Trixie is related to me and Boomer. We aren't close, but I think she does that intentionally. She must miss Hawk fiercely not to want to be around her family. I can't blame her. If Reaper ever died, I think I'd want to be alone too. Being around everyone that knew him and loved him would be too hard to handle.

Shaking my head to get out of the depressing thought, I peel back the tissue paper and pick up the red top. It's leather with white fuzzy cups for my breasts to mimic a

A RUTHLESS CHRISTMAS

Santa outfit. The panties are leather too, but there is something special about them I think he'll like.

They're crotchless.

My cheeks heat from the reaction I'm imagining in my head from Reaper. After everything we've shared in the bedroom, I can't believe I still blush. He makes me feel so innocent all the time, and the sex gets better with every thrust.

Oh wow, it just got hot in here. I fan myself and take a deep breath. I don't know why I get so nervous every time I dress up for him. I know he loves me mor than anything, but a small part of me always thinks he won't like it.

"Doll, you okay in there?" He knocks on the door, and my heart leaps up to my throat. I hold the top to my chest and close my eyes, taking a deep breath. "Is your stomach okay? Are you in pain?"

And then my heart drops back to my chest when I feel his love seep through the door. He's been worried sick about my wound healing. Every now and then I get a sharp pain, but I'm fine. There's no reason to tell anyone about it.

"I'm fine," I finally speak up. "Did Doc bandage you up from the wild swamp kitty attack?" I giggle at my joke. Reaper can be such a baby sometimes, which is hilarious, since he's the most badass man I've ever met in my life.

"I'm fine," he huffs. "'Tis but a flesh wound," he quotes in an accent from Monty Python and the Holy Grail movie we watched the other night.

He says the damn sentence every chance he gets now. It's adorable, but somehow, he relates it to everything.

"I'll be out in a minute," I say, taking off my top to get the show on the road.

"Okay, Doll, I'll be waiting for you. I thought we could go for a ride today? It'll be cold, but the day is pretty."

Oh, we're going for a ride alright. Just not the kind he's expecting. "Sure, baby. That's sounds good."

"I'll wait for you out here."

Yeah, we aren't going anywhere.

I slip the leather bra under my breasts, then spin it around and hook my arms through the straps. Wow, it's tight. My eyebrows reach my hairline in appreciation. My boobs are pushed up as high as they can go. Damn, they look good. I run my fingers through the white fuzz along the hem of the cups as the red leather shines in the light of the bathroom.

I slip off my pants and panties next, but before I can put on the second half of Reaper's surprise, a sharp pain ignites through the scar on my abdomen. I double over, catching myself on the edge of the sink. It's like Tongue's knife is stabbing me all over again. I breathe in through my nose and out through my mouth, then just like that, it's gone.

I finish dressing, then grab the pair of black thigh-high leather boots and pull them on. Thinking about Reaper already has me wet and aching. I fluff my hair by flipping it over and running my fingers through it. Next, I put on some cherry lip gloss and smirk at myself in the mirror.

Oh yeah, the only place we're going is the bed.

I open the door and see that he has his back to me. He's in briefs, changing his clothes to get ready for the bike ride he thinks we're going on, and his shoulders flex as he digs through the dresser drawers.

God, he's fucking sexy.

A RUTHLESS CHRISTMAS

I lean against the wall, stick my leg out, and clear my throat.

"Have you seen my Ruthless Kings shirt? The one with the hole in the armpit? I know, I need to toss it, but it's my favorite."

"Yeah, I'm wearing it," I lie, but it has him turning around, showing off his impressive eight-pack abs. He's so sexy. I love that he's getting some more gray around his temples too. A gush of hot liquid leaves me as I stare at him, eating him up from head to toe.

I don't miss the noticeable bulge in his underwear. The big, thick, bulge that my pussy was made for.

He doesn't say a word. He is speechless.

"I was wondering, Jesse," I purr his name which has him gripping his cock. "Have you been naughty?" I rub my hands down my torso seductively, then up again, grabbing my breasts. "Or nice?"

He growls, then charges toward me in loud, pounding footsteps. He wraps a strong arm around my waist and picks me up. My legs wrap around his hips, and my crotchless panties rub against him, soaking his briefs with the lust he causes me to feel. He senses something different and slides one hand between us, dipping his fingers through my exposed folds.

"I've been real fucking naughty," he rumbles, sinking two fingers inside of me.

I moan, a jaw-dropping sensation taking over my body as he pumps into me, preparing me for the long, thick intrusion he's about to give me.

"You're never allowed to wear anything else ever again." He brings his hand from between my legs and stuffs the two fingers in my mouth. I let my tongue wrap around his thick digits, letting the sweet nectar slide down my throat. He loves it when I taste myself. "Looks like I'm not the only one who's been naughty," he says with hooded eyes as I suck his fingers like I would his cock.

He holds me by the meat of my ass and carries me to the bed in two steps. The soft comforter hits my back, and I sink into the soft pillowtop of the mattress. Reaper appreciates my body, slinking his hands up and down every curve before parting my legs. He closes his eyes when he sees me, then licks his lips. He takes my left ankle and places it on top of his shoulder, then does the same with my right.

His shaggy hair hangs in his face as he rubs his cheeks against the leather boots while staring at my pussy. Reaper slides up while wrapping my legs around his waist and finally kisses me. His lips always surprise me because they're so much softer than they look. Our tongues meet and lick one another before he takes my bottom lip into his mouth, then he runs his palms over my breasts. We groan into each other's mouths as my palms wraps around his scorching hot steel.

I push down his briefs just below his ass and guide him to my entrance. Every inch of me is on fire, and I need him to extinguish it.

"In a hurry?" I can feel the smirk of his lips stretching across mine just as the wide tip of his cock settles inside me.

"I need you," I moan. My clit throbs, my nipples are tight beads, and if he doesn't get inside me right now, I think I might die.

Is that possible? To die of not being fucked properly? It has to be.

A RUTHLESS CHRISTMAS

He curls his hands around my shoulders, then pushes me down and thrusts forward at the same time. "Oh, yes!" I shout in relief as all of his thick, delicious inches fill me up.

"Fuck, Doll. So wet, so tight," he murmurs against the side of my neck. My nails drift down his shoulders, scratching down his back until I'm squeezing the firm globes of his ass. He pulls out, then thrusts inside again, leaving me gasping and that much closer to an orgasm.

He picks up the pace and lifts off me, staring at where we're connected. "This cunt is mine, Doll."

"All yours, Jesse. All yours." I drop my arms behind my head and stretch them out, getting lost in the sensations he's giving me. No one could ever make me feel as loved, appreciated, and sexy like Reaper does. He never makes me feel unwanted. If anything, sometimes I think his love for me hurts with how he looks at me and touches me. It's as if he can't get enough and that's what every woman in a relationship wants to feel.

"That's right," he growls, gripping the headboard behind us. He loves doing that. The more leverage he can get, the deeper and harder he can fill me. "My fucking pussy, my fucking body." He lays his hand over my heart and rocks his head back. "Mine."

"Yes," I moan as my orgasm approaches. "Yes!" A fever rushes in my veins as my belly flips and turns.

"Come for me, Doll. Come all over my cock," he orders.

I drop my hand between my legs to rub my clit, but he slaps it away, and the slight sting has me whimpering for more.

"You're going to come because of me and me alone. Understand?"

I nod, stretching my hands on either side of me and grip the sheets. I'm holding myself back. The pressure builds in the lower half of my body, and my breath catches in my ribcage.

"That's it. I feel that cunt wanting to release. Come on, Doll. Milk me," he says. Reaper brings his lips to my ear. "I want every drop of my seed inside you."

Thinking about finally having his baby tips me over the edge. "Jesse! Yes, so good," I shout, my entire body tensing as waves of sheer ecstasy pump through me at the same rhythm of his cock.

He groans, tossing his head back until the tendons are thick and protruding. His hands fall from the headboard and grab onto my tits with a painful squeeze, but I love it. I always love when he feels so good his pleasure brings pain.

In three rough thrusts of his hips, he plants himself inside me, trying to shove deeper inside me with every jet of cum. I milk him just like he told me to, hoping that one finally takes root. I want nothing more than to have his child.

Just one.

If I can have just one…

"Sarah," he grunts my name through a held breath and a red face as he pours everything he has into my womb.

Like he does every time.

He collapses on top of me but catches enough of his weight on his forearms, so he doesn't squish me to death. Reaper's cock spasms the last of his orgasm and he moans, capturing my mouth in a heated, yet gentle kiss.

His gigantic palm lands on my belly, and I know he's hoping something happens from this. I'm not holding my

A RUTHLESS CHRISTMAS

breath. It hasn't happened, and it will probably never happen, but no matter what, he's going to love me through it.

"I know what you're thinking," he says, breaking the kiss. We gasp for air, and the heat of his breath puffs against my chin. The room smells of sex, sweat, and cum.

And a hint of sadness.

"It's going to happen," he states with endless determination.

I wrap my arms around his neck and bring his head closer again to kiss the man I love. I don't want to get lost in despair right now. I want to be lost in Jesse, my heart's reaper. Our tongues intertwine tenderly, and he runs his fingers softly through my hair, pouring every ounce of love he has into it. I don't know how long we lay there kissing one another, but he slowly starts moving again.

It isn't rough.

It isn't hurried.

It isn't desperate.

He makes love to me, and I let him.

CHAPTER THREE

Juliette

We're only open for a few more days before we close for Christmas Day. We're debating staying open for Christmas Eve for all the lost souls that wander in off the streets, alone with no place to go. It sounds like a good thing to do, even if it is only one person, but we also want to be home with our Ruthless Kings family.

If I know Tool like I think I do, he's going to decide to keep Kings' Club open. On the inside, he's a big softy.

And he never stops being sexy.

"Damn it!" he shouts in pain for the hundredth time from across the stage. He's hanging mistletoe.

Everywhere.

He says if everyone has to stop and kiss every few feet, no one a reason to go home alone.

I think he's about to give up because it's the fourth time he's hit his thumb with the hammer. It isn't his tool of choice.

My man is good with a screwdriver, but a hammer? He might end up killing himself if he isn't careful.

"You okay, sweetheart?" I yell, wrapping the garland around the vintage microphone.

"Fine," he grumbles. "'Tis but a flesh wound."

I roll my eyes from the quote. Him and Reaper can't seem to stop watching that damn movie. I'm about to call Boomer and have him blow up that damn DVD. Every single copy ever made. I'm sure he'd appreciate the challenge.

"Do you want me to kiss it to make it better?"

The hammer clatters to the ground, and his boots slam on the floor as he jumps down from the ladder. I don't even have to look away from what I'm doing to know he's on his way over. A black and blue thumb is shoved in front of me, and I gasp from how horrible it looks. I wrap my fingers around his wrist and gape. "Tool, I didn't know it was this bad. We might need to see Doc."

"I'm fine. It's just bruised."

"It looks broken." I twist and turn his hand, trying to look at it from every angle. I'm learning a lot about medicine from Doc, and I help out when I can because the poor man does so much for everyone when they're injured, and I know he gets overwhelmed.

"Well, it wouldn't be if you'd kiss it."

"Oh yeah?" I purr, adjusting my knees on the stage. I bring his abused thumb to my lips and press a kiss to it. "That better?"

His nostrils flare. "A little more."

The damn screwdriver behind his ear is getting the space between my legs wet. I love how he protects me with it, what

A RUTHLESS CHRISTMAS

he has done to make sure I'm here with him. There isn't anything hotter than a man, especially a man like Tool, defending you. He's muscular, tattooed from head to toe, and don't get me started on his cock.

It's huge, pierced, and always gets the job done.

And he needs to get to work on me because we're the only two here. The club doesn't open for another hour, and with how my eyes are level with the growing bulge in his pants, if I don't get a taste, my Christmas might be damned.

I roll my tongue over his thumb, licking it like I would his cock, and he grumbles. Wrapping my lips around the digit, I bob my head up and down, then stop. "Better?" I ask, my voice hoarse with arousal.

"Almost," he says, unzipping his pants. He's about to pull out that big, beautiful beast when an urgent knock on the door stops him. Tool's hand is inside his pants, most likely wrapped around his cock. "No! No, no, no. We can ignore them. They will go away."

But the pounding continues. It's desperate and fast.

"Son of a bitch," Tool gripes, zipping his pants in anger. He grabs my chin and forces me to meet his chocolate brown eyes. "You aren't going anywhere. I expect those lips around my cock to make my thumb better."

"I forgot your thumb was connected to your dick." I chuckle.

"Little sparrow, every part of my body is connected to my cock when it comes to you." He slams his mouth on mine and his new tongue piercing massages the inside of my mouth which has me whimpering with more need. That damn person at the door better be bleeding.

His tongue untangles itself from mine, leaving me wondering how the hell this is my life and how I have a man like Tool.

I watch his perky ass walk away from me, and I hurry to fix my hair, so I don't look like a sex fiend. I get back to wrapping the garland around the microphone. I'm hot all over. I knew I shouldn't have worn long sleeves today. Tool always makes my temperature rise.

"Juliette! Get some blankets from the back, now!" Tool yells, and I jump from the stage when I see him carrying a woman who is battered and bruised all over. Her lips are blue, and her skin is pale. I don't question him. I run through the club and dash through the purple velvet curtain. The pitter patter of my feet echo off the walls as I hurry to his office.

It's still the only part of the club that has yet to be renovated. We've been too busy to worry about it. I yank the door open and rush toward the closet in the back. I flip on the light and grab as many blankets as I can, including a heated one. If people aren't from Vegas, they don't know, or maybe consider how cold it can get in the desert. This girl looks like she's been in the cold for days.

And if the Ruthless Kings' history is anything to go by, it means bad shit is coming our way.

We will handle it. We always do.

Or maybe we will get lucky and this is some random girl, who just needs a little help getting on her feet, and is not lost, or getting abused, or homeless.

Christmas miracles happen, right?

I run out the door and down the hall, hugging the blankets to my chest. I push the curtain open, and Tool has her laid on the stage. He gently lifts her head up to tuck a pillow under her; he must have got it from one of the couches in the corner. "Here, I grabbed a heated blanket too."

"Perfect," he says, unfolding the electric blanket and throwing it over the frail woman. There's an outlet right beneath us, and he plugs in the cord and cranks the heat up to high. Luckily, we have outlets everywhere. We never thought they would be used for this though. Through the day, we serve brunch and coffee, and we get a lot of business from college kids and hungover partiers.

"My gosh, she's so cold." I touch her hand, then wrap my fingers around the side of her palm. Her entire body shivers, and her teeth clatter together. Her eyes are closed, but they're moving behind her eyelids quickly. "Miss?" I try to nudge her awake. "Miss, what happened to you? Can you hear me?" I try saying, knowing it's a longshot, but we have no idea what to do right now. Her clothes are thin, worn, and with plenty of holes. Her shoes are old, the soles barely hanging on, and she's filthy. Her hair is matted, her lips are chapped, and she's so damn skinny.

I can tell, even underneath all the mess and dirt, she's beautiful.

"Go get some water," I tell Tool, but he's already reaching for his phone in his pocket.

"We have to call 911. Maybe they can help her," Tool says, but her hand suddenly grips his wrist so tight, his skin turns white.

"No," she croaks, licking her dry lips. "No hospitals. Please," she wheezes. "Jesse. Get Jesse." She opens her eyes, and Tool inhales a sharp breath that sucks all the air out of the room. The woman's eyes flutter shut, and Tool just stares at her, open-mouthed and wide-eyed.

"What is it?" I ask, but he doesn't hear me. "Logan!" I make sure there is emphasis on his name, so it pulls him out of the trance he's in. "What's going on?"

He blinks, his lush black lashes fanning over his face as he prepares for what he's about to say. The damn anticipation is killing me. "What?" I ask again, getting impatient. He knows something. "Logan, out with it. We have an hour before we open, and we have a half dead woman on the stage."

"I think…" He runs his fingers through his hair. "I think she's asking for Reaper."

"Okay?" I say, not understanding where he's going with this. "A lot of people come to the Kings if they need help, right?"

"Yeah, but most of it is money situations. People owe us a lot of money, but Reaper stays on top of it."

"I didn't know that."

"It isn't that important compared to all the other things that have happened."

"So what, you think she owes money?"

"No. She doesn't need that kind of help. I think she's asking for Reaper because this woman, whoever she is, is his daughter."

"Shut the hell up!" I squeal so loud my voice echoes, and Tool throws his hands over his ears. "Are you sure?"

"Not completely, but they look so much alike; it's hard to deny the facts."

"I don't think they look that much alike," I say, tilting my head as I examine her face. Same nose, but she has bigger lips,

A RUTHLESS CHRISTMAS

sharp jawline like Reaper, brown eyes, dirty blonde hair, but that isn't evidence. "Plenty of people have similar features."

"And the people who have similar features don't just go around asking for someone who looks a lot like them."

That's a valid point.

"She's young."

"So is Sarah," he argues.

Another valid point.

"If that's true, things are about to get awkward."

"I just hope I'm wrong because if he has a daughter while Reaper and Sarah are trying to get pregnant, Sarah will feel like he doesn't need her anymore."

I hope Logan is wrong, but the more I look at the woman on stage, the more I think he's right.

CHAPTER FOUR

Reaper

"**M**Y MAZE, WAKE UP." I NUDGE MY LITTLE GIRL'S ARM gently as she sleeps. It's kind of late, but I'll be damned if I miss one more day to make her excited for Christmas. I've been a bad dad; I haven't tried hard enough to make Christmas special for her. That changes now, though, because it's the first holiday she's spent here since she was rescued, and she deserves to feel all the Christmas cheer.

I also shouldn't think of her as my daughter. Nothing is finalized. If anyone ever found out we had her, we would probably be charged with kidnapping. Badge dug into the missing persons database, but since we don't know her last name, there was only a few hundred pictures to look through because her name is so unique.

What we found had me begging to kill her father, who is currently in prison for sexually assaulting her younger brother. I don't know where he is; we have looked everywhere. I just hope her father didn't sell him to the same people that had my Maze. Her mother is dead, so we are the only real family she has.

Are we fucking dipped in gold?

No.

But we don't hurt innocent people. We don't fucking hurt kids. She's safe here. I'll fucking climb all the mountains, kill all the people, and slay all of the dragons if it means keeping her safe. Someone hadn't tried hard enough before, but that's not the case now.

She has more than a dozen men at her side, her army, and nothing is going to get in the way of us fighting all of her battles. Even when she's grown. And I don't care what I need to do, what laws I need to break—Maze will be here with us. She will have my last name, and she will be my little girl.

It's the only way I know she will be protected. We can give her the love she deserves. She's so different from me and Sarah. It's obvious she isn't our biological child, but it feels like it. Maze has long dark hair and big brown doe eyes with long lashes that nearly touch her brow. When she's older, she's going to be gorgeous.

You know how many souls I'm going to have to reap then? Stupid fucking boys. I know what they want, and they sure as hell aren't going to come near my Maze trying to get it.

Her lashes flutter, and those beautiful brown irises blink at me. "Dadd—

I mean, Reaper," she corrects herself, and I have to hold my breath to stop the pure fucking joy and emotion coursing through me right now.

I clear my throat and hold back the burn behind my eyes,

A RUTHLESS CHRISTMAS

so I don't lose it. I'm the Prez. I can't lose it. I have to be strong for everyone a hundred times over because that's what Presidents do—they find strength when none is left.

"Hey, Maze. Just letting you know, you can call me Daddy, or Reaper, or Jesse. I'm happy with any of them." I try to play it cool, but I really want her to call me Daddy. I never once thought I'd have the chance, but yet, here I am.

And I've never wanted it more.

"Okay," she whispers and stretches her arms up and over her head as she yawns, showing her two front teeth that are missing.

Shut the fuck up! No kid is allowed to be this fucking cute.

"You want to go get that tree we've been talking about?" I ask her.

I've never seen anyone move so fast in my life. She bolts out of bed, tripping on the comforter that's wrapped around her foot, but I catch her so she doesn't fall. She's wearing a onesie that has those Disney Frozen princesses all over it. She puts on her bunny slippers, then her Trolls beanie and grabs her puffy white jacket that makes her look like a marshmallow. Maze is ready in less than a minute.

It's impressive, but getting the girl to brush her teeth … that can take an eternity.

"You sure you want to go?" I ask her, and she grabs my hand to drag me out the door.

"I'm sure. I'm sure. I'm sure! Let's go, Daddy. Let's go!"

She decided to call me Daddy.

I wipe my right eye on my shirt sleeve. Allergies. Presidents of a badass MC do not cry.

"Anything you fucking want, Maze." I smile, lifting her up by her arms and hitching her to my side.

"You said a bad word," she calls me out. "I'm gonna tell Mommy."

She's got to stop. I can't take it anymore. Maybe it's because Sarah and I have been trying so hard to have kids, and hearing the title hits home. "Badge, watch Maze for a second; I need to go find Sarah," I say, handing Maze off to the guy who can't stand children but loves Maze.

He holds her out in front of him, hands under her armpits, and looking unsure of what to do. "Um, okay. I can do it. I got it."

"I'm not an *it*!" Maze harrumphs, crossing her arms over her chest.

"You're something," Badge comments as I walk away, which makes me smile to myself.

She really is something.

Before I find Sarah, I need a minute. Right now, I don't want to be Reaper. I don't want to be the President of the Ruthless Kings.

I want to be a dad. For the first time in my life, I'm a fucking dad. I slink into the kitchen without bothering to turn on any lights and grab the edge of the table to stop myself from falling over.

In happiness.

In exhaustion.

In relief.

And I allow myself to tear up. I knock my knuckles on the table, harder than I intended, and let myself feel the immense joy in my heart right now. No one can relate except

A RUTHLESS CHRISTMAS

Sarah. God, we've been trying and trying and fucking trying to get pregnant. I don't have the strength to tell Sarah that I don't think it will happen. We lost the one we were meant to have, and for a long time I held out hope, but every time she takes a pregnancy test and she cries, I lose a little bit of that hope I've been clinging onto.

But now, I swear to God, my heart is fucking full.

"Ye alright, Prez? I swear, I hear sniffles," Skirt says from behind me, carrying his newborn daughter, Joey, named after Doc's ol' lady, Joanna after she tried to save Skirt's life from a fire.

"I'm fine." That sounds like a lie. My voice cracks, completely giving away how I'm doing.

"Shite, Prez. What the fuck happened? Is Sarah okay? Is Maizey okay? Did someone die? Damn it, don't tell me someone died."

I push Skirt by the shoulder until we are safe in the hallway where my office is. "Maizey called me Daddy," I say proudly, nearly puffing out my chest. "I'm a Dad."

Skirt's eyes soften around the edges as he stares at me. In a flash of understanding, he knows that right now I'm not trying to be tough. I'm not trying to be the man everyone needs me to be all the time. I'm fucking human at the end of the day, and I won't blink an eye when it comes to killing necessary evil. But when it comes to the ones I love, I have a soft spot in my heart. An area of quicksand that I get lost in when I'm around Sarah or Maizey.

"Aye, Reaper. Yer a dad. Bring it in, big fella. Congratulations." He gives me a quick hug and pats me on the back, and we're careful not to squish Joey between us.

"Thank you." Being soft, I place my arm on his throat and push him against the wall, so quick, yet gentle so I don't wake his daughter. "If you tell anyone about this, I'll be fucking furious."

"Ye don't want to tell people yer a dad?"

"No one knows I teared up. Got it?"

"Ah, aye, got it. Don't worry, Reaper. I don't think less of ye for dropping a few tears. Being a dad does that. I can't go anywhere without my Joey. I feel fucking lost when she isn't attached to me. I got to feel her little breaths and hear those tiny sighs. Her fist likes to grip on to me beard and yank it. It hurts, and I'll forever have a few bald patches, but I wouldn't trade her for the world."

I let go of his neck, and he brings Joey up to his shoulder, burying his nose in her bright red hair. She's Skirt's daughter, that's for sure.

"That's so sweet," Tongue's drawl comes from a nearby corner, but I don't know which.

It has me and Skirt jumping, and I don't find it to be a coincidence that Joey starts to cry. "Damn it, Tongue."

"Congratulations, Reaper. I'm happy for you." And just like that, the scary bastard is gone.

I reach my hand into the corner and grab nothing but air. He was here, though. He was right here.

"Shhh, it's okay. Tongue isn't going to get ye, baby. I got ye." Skirt bounces to hush his little girl to keep her from crying, but she isn't letting up anytime soon. She gets louder. "Damn it, Tongue."

"I plan on getting the tree. Do you, Dawn, Aidan, and little miss thing here want to go?"

A RUTHLESS CHRISTMAS

"Aye. Let me tell Dawn and Aidan."

"Reaper! Reaper!" Tool's voice is urgent as he yells out my name.

I turn to look over my shoulder to see him dart through the kitchen, searching for me. I step out of the hallway and flip on the light. He stops in his tracks, and shakes his head at me as I start unsheathing the knife I keep tucked away in the back of my pants. "What happened?"

"No, you don't need that," he gasps, the light shining against the sweat on his forehead. "A woman came into the club. She's in bad shape. She's in the main room, and Doc is looking her over."

"Oh." I put my knife away and start toward the main room. "Is she okay? What's her name?"

"I don't know, but she asked for you."

"Uh, interesting. Okay, I'll go check it out."

Tool's hand stops me by gripping my bicep. "Prez, I have to warn you. She looks a lot like you. And she's young."

I think about what he's saying and hope like hell Tool doesn't mean what I think he means. "You might want to cut to the chase before you piss me off and ruin my good mood."

"Just go see for yourself. I'm probably wrong."

My heart thumps as I stomp my way down the hallway. When I come through, Badge is there, still holding Maizey as if she has a disease.

"I can do this all day, buddy," Maizey says, poking Badge in the cheek.

"I hope not," he mumbles under his breath.

I don't have time to deal with that right now. I have to

go see what the fuss is about. I get to the living room, and Doc is listening to the stranger's heartbeat, while the guys hover around as close as they can.

The expression on their faces tells me I need to be worried. When Poodle's eyes meet mine, and he swallows. I look to Slingshot next to him, who pops a skittle in his mouth, but won't even meet my eyes. Knives is spinning his ninja start in his hand while Mary is on the other side of him, sitting in a chair, still healing from a piece of wood impaling her leg. She kicks Knives, and he drops his ninja star on the ground, which rolls to the tip of my boot.

Clink.

The steel-toe of my boot meets the silver star, and it causes it to tip over.

"You made me drop my star, Mary!"

"Maybe you aren't as slick with your weapon as you thought."

"Want to find out?" he challenges her, and even though I'm in the room, they won't look at me either.

Fuck.

My phone vibrates in my pocket, and I pull it out; it's Boomer calling. Damn it, he probably wants to talk about Christmas plans.

But there's always something, isn't there? Can't we have a fucking month where nothing happens? I'd love for the only thing I need to be worried about is Tongue blindly making people mute and Slingshot's taco disorder because it sure as fuck is not an addiction.

I ignore his call and squat next to Doc in front of the couch. I analyze the woman. She's skinny. Her clothes are old, and she smells like she hasn't bathed in weeks. "What've we got?"

"I wish I knew more, but I don't. She's coming out of hypothermia, which is odd. It's cold, but it isn't that cold. It's like she walked out of a freezer to get to this state. She's skinny, and the poor girl has been through it. She's bruised all over, a few cuts, fractured orbital socket. I'd put her in her early twenties, maybe nineteen? She's young."

"Jesse," she whispers my name, and I fall onto my ass in surprise.

I point at her. "I've never met this woman in my life. She can't be going around saying my name like that. Sarah will kill her."

The girl starts to come to, pinching her brows in pain before her eyes open, and they're the same color as mine. She searches her surroundings, and our eyes lock, and something snaps into place. I don't know what it is, but I have this need to take care of her. "Jesse," she says my name again, but it's weighed down with so much pain. Her eyes water, and the first of her tears fall. "I found you."

I knee-walk to her and take her hand in mine. "Listen, you've got to tell me how we know each other because I can't remember. I'm an asshole like that," I state, which causes her to smile. It's watery and tired, but it's there.

"What's going on?" Sarah asks as she walks around the couch. When she sees me holding the hand of another woman, she doesn't think twice or doubt me. She knows I would never set my eyes on anyone else, and I love her for it. She lays her hand on top of mine and the person she doesn't know. "Are you okay? Oh my God. What happened?"

"What's your name?" I ask her, squeezing her hand to keep her awake. "How do you know me?"

"My mom said." Her teeth clatter against one another, and she gives a full body shiver.

"Give me another damn blanket!" I bark.

Not two seconds later, the guest in our house is covered in ten of them. I'm going to leave them there. She seems like she needs all the heat.

She tries again, stammering through the shivers. "My mom … said if anything … bad ever happened to … to find you, Jesse. Vegas. Ruthless Kings." She repeats the last three as if reading from a list in her mind. "Jesse. Vegas. Ruthless Kings," she says again.

"Hey, you're here," I say, cupping her jaw with my hand, but she flinches away. "I'm sorry. I didn't mean to hurt you."

"Delilah," she stammers. "My name is Delilah."

"That's a pretty name," I say, staring into her eyes that are eerily similar to mine. "Are you my daughter? I swear to God, I didn't know about you," I blurt.

She chuckles before painfully groaning, then shakes her head. "Sister," she corrects me.

"Sister? That's … no. That's impossible." It isn't. My dad wasn't a saint. He fucked around with club sluts every single day until the day he died.

But the longer I stare into her eyes, the more I know she's right. They're too familiar. The structure of her face, her mouth, the color of her hair; even the way she smiles is too much like me. I don't need details when the facts are staring me in the face.

A RUTHLESS CHRISTMAS

I have a sister.
And she's under the Kings protection now.
Until death.
And after.
It's the Ruthless way.

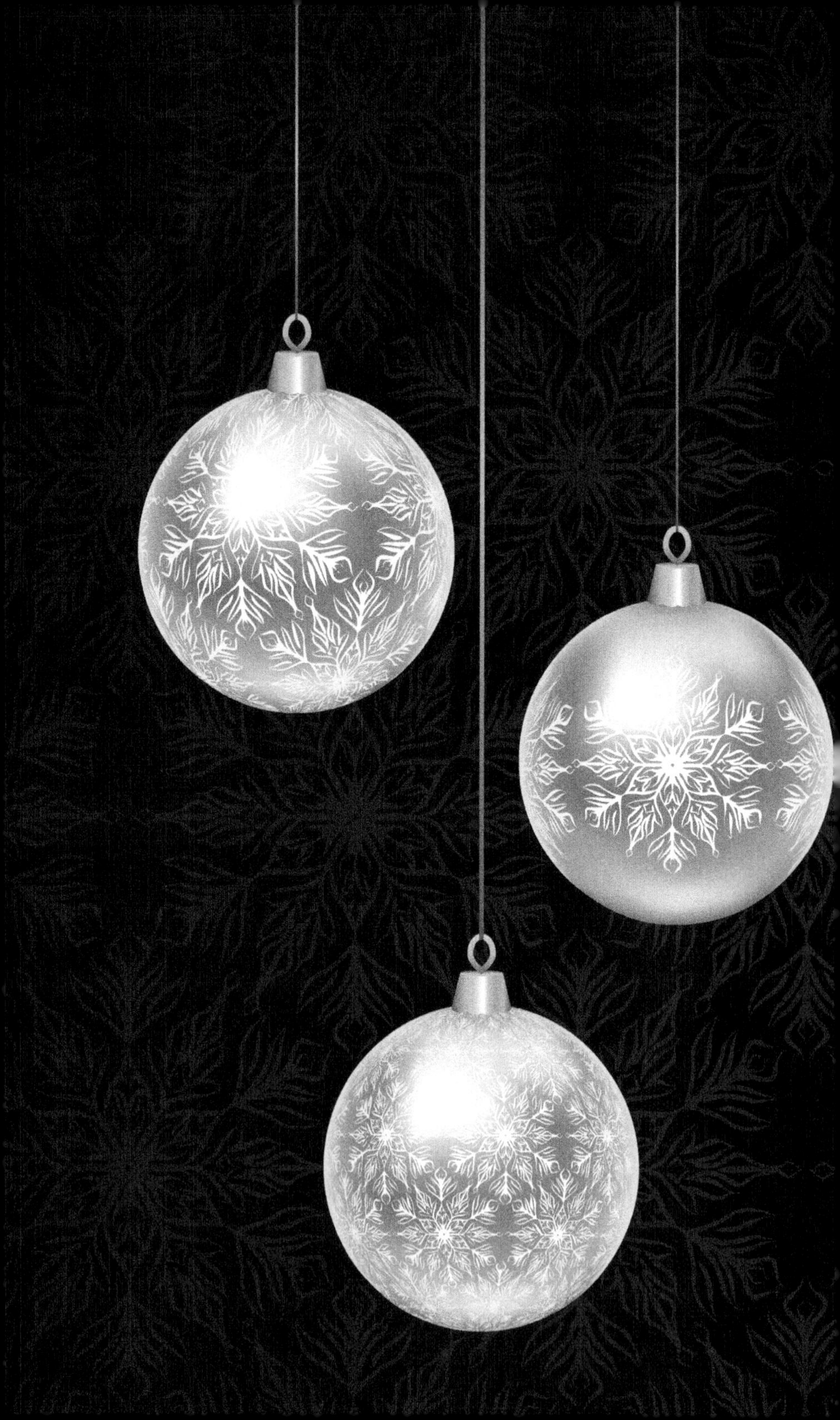

CHAPTER FIVE

Sarah

DELILAH IS ASLEEP. MAIZEY FELL ASLEEP IN BADGE'S ARMS right there on the floor. They finally gave up whatever power trip they were on. Everyone might be asleep, but Jesse is wide awake. We haven't made our way home yet. The clubhouse isn't where we sleep anymore. We have a cabin on the property, but we've somehow been staying here more since everything has happened. I wouldn't be surprised if Reaper moved us back in temporarily.

He's sitting in Church at the head of the table on his throne. The chair is new, made up of black leather and hand-carved skulls surrounding the frame. The power he has in that chair vibrates my body. He's holding the gavel, staring at it as if he's waiting for it to grow the body it used to belong to. It's old, older than him and his father, along with this table.

Bad things happen in this room.

Deadly decisions are made, but sometimes, Reaper needs the room to think.

He isn't sitting in the chair normally. He's leaned against the side, one leg up and bent. One elbow is on his knee while the other is on the arm of the chair, rolling the human bone in his hand.

"You okay?" I ask him, knocking slightly on the door to let him know I'm here.

He gives an easy shake of the head, then lifts his eyes to look at me. I hate seeing him in so much pain. I'm the only one who ever gets to see it, and it kills me every time. "How did I not know about her, Doll?" he asks, hoping that I hold all the answers in the world. "She can't be older than you."

"Does…" I'm trying to untwist the knife in my gut from how his tone sounds. "Does that bother you?"

"What? No, it has nothing to do with that, Doll. You little maniac. You know I don't give a damn about our age difference."

"Anymore," I tease him.

"You were jailbait."

"Yeah, I was, wasn't I?" I giggle. "I was such a brat."

"Was?"

"You better watch it." I'm hoping our teasing back and forth helps his mood. I close the door behind me, taking one last look at Maizey and Badge on the floor. His arms are tucked behind his head, and she's curled up in a ball next to him. The dogs surround them too. Yeti, Tyrant, Chaos, and Lady. Lady isn't as healthy as she used to be. Poodle is worried this will be her last Christmas, which will fucking kill him and everyone else. Lady means the world to everyone.

A RUTHLESS CHRISTMAS

Once the door clicks shut, I make my way over to Reaper and take the gavel from him, setting it on the table that has the Ruthless Kings MC emblem carved in the middle of it. "Then what is it?" I say, keeping my voice almost as low as a whisper. I run my hands through his shaggy hair, which is a bit oily from the day, and it makes the strands slide between my fingers easier. Plus, the unkempt greasy look is sexy on him. When he is fresh out of the Kings' Garage? He can't get me off him.

"She's around your age, Doll. If what Doc said is true, how did I go nearly twenty years without knowing she existed? What's happened to her wouldn't have happened if she would've been here with me. I never expected to know how Boomer felt after meeting you, and now I do. I feel like I've been punched in the gut, and I'm angry at the world for not telling me about Delilah. She's hurt. She's scared. She was nearly frozen to death. Who did that to her?" He curls his lip in and slams his fist on the table, the gavel teetering on its end. "I want to find them, rip their hearts from their chest, and let her watch the worthless organ pump in my fist. I want her to know she's safe."

I straddle his waist, and he moves his legs down between mine so I can be more comfortable. There's one thing that can never be argued when it comes to Reaper, and that is how passionate he is. He takes his title very seriously. This isn't a job to him; this is his family. There isn't a better man to be President of the Ruthless Kings.

"You're going to keep her safe. She's only been here for an hour. She's home now. She's never been more protected than she is now."

"I know that … I know. I'm just…" He sighs and tightens a hand around my waist. I snuggle against his chest, laying my cheek against his defined pec as I rub up and down his arms. "I'm shocked. God, I thought she was my daughter. What would you have done if you'd found out I had a daughter your age?"

I sit up and cup the side of his face. His beard scratches the palm of my hand, and his skin is softer than anyone would expect. He has a few wrinkles around his eyes from squinting so much, and the gray around his temples checks all my damn boxes. I make sure his browns meet mine. His are darker, nearly obsidian and blending into his pupils. It's hard to tell what's what some days depending on how the light hits them.

"I would have loved you just as much and probably more than I do today, Jesse. It wouldn't have bothered me if you had a daughter. I'm not oblivious to the life you lived before me. I know with our age difference comes experiences you have that I don't. I would have loved you, and I would have loved her."

"I just thought with us trying so hard, maybe it would take away from us, and I didn't want you to feel slighted."

"Baby," I exhale. "Never would anything take away from that. Nothing. If you have a sister today and three daughters walk through the door tomorrow, I'd still want you to lay me down at night and make love to me because I would still want to have your baby."

He hums in agreement, rubbing his hand over my stomach. His eyebrows do that worrying frown in the middle. I know exactly what he's thinking right now, but I don't want to talk about that. "I don't know how to be a brother," he says after a few minutes of silence.

"I'm sure she doesn't know how to be a sister either, but she came here knowing her brother would protect her. That means something, doesn't it? Already, there's a bond."

He slithers his hands between mine and places each palm on either side of my neck. His thumbs stroke down the curve of my neck, and I close my eyes, tilting back to give him more access. "I fucking love you, you know that?" he asks, skimming his hands down my front and cupping my breasts.

"Reaper, we can't do it here," I moan, rocking my hips against his erection pressing against my center.

"Your support turns me the fuck on. I need you now, Doll."

"We can't." I gasp when his lips land on the side of my neck, sucking one of his famous marks he likes to leave on me.

"I'm the President. I get to do whatever the fuck I want, when I want, where the hell I want." He unbuttons my jeans and dips his hand under my panties, his fingers brushing through the trimmed blonde tuft. My jaw drops when his index finger presses against my swollen clit. "I get to touch my ol' lady's cunt whenever I want; isn't that right?" he asks, nibbling down my neck. He licks the edge of my collarbone, and my skin pebbles with excitement.

"Yes," I hiss, rocking my hips for more friction.

"Prez!" Patrick knocks.

I sag against Reaper's body and bite the muscle of his shoulder into my mouth. I have to do my best not to cry out in rage; I'm so worked up.

"This better be fucking good, Patrick. Speak," Reaper barks, still rolling my clit slowly, and with every complete circle, my body jerks and my teeth dig further into his shoulder.

"Remember that guy I met in rehab? Loch? Him and his sister are here."

"Sisters are dropping from the sky today," Reaper mumbles, pulling his hand out of my pants with disappointment. He drops his forehead on my shoulder. "Sorry, Doll. I got to go."

"I know." I claw my nails into his shoulder as I try to gain control of myself. "I want you so bad."

He growls, picking me up and placing me on the table. "You're testing every ounce of my control. You have no idea how much I want to lay you down and fuck you right here."

"Real quick. Make them wait," I beg, pulling off my shirt and throwing it against the wall. I unhook my bra, which luckily snaps in front, and the material falls to the side.

I know I have Reaper hook, line, and sinker when he sees me half naked.

He takes his time dragging his hands over my flat, scarred stomach. He tweaks my nipples, poking his tongue from between his lips as he tugs on the red peaks. I bend my back and dig my nails into the old wood grain of the table from the sensations.

"You're nothing but trouble," Reaper growls, giving the beads a hard twist, which has me gasping for air.

"What are you going to do about it?" I fire back, challenging him, hoping that he makes them wait outside because I need him so much it hurts.

He unbuttons my jeans, unzips my pants, then tugs them

A RUTHLESS CHRISTMAS

down to my knees. "I'm going to fill you with my cock, use that sweet cunt, leave my cum in you, and then go take care of business." He slaps my ass as he takes a leg in each hand and flips me onto my stomach.

"Yes," I hiss, pushing my cheek into the table.

I hear the delicious sound of his zipper and then the cool air breezing over my wet heat. His finger pushes the annoying material of the panties aside, and then in one thrust, he's settled inside me. He wraps my hair around his wrist and yanks me up, so my back is flush with his front. Reaper nibbles on my ear, pushing another inch inside me, and I pulsate around him, already close to the edge.

"I love how wet you get for me. This is going to be quick, Doll. I want to fill you so bad." His dirty whispered words have my clit throbbing between my legs.

I place two fingers on the swollen bundle and quake as the sensitivity overflows through every nerve of my body..

"Hold on tight, Doll," he warns me as one hand grips my left hip and the other stays locked in my hair. His cock stretches me as he pulls out, then roughly shoves back in. His pace is quick, hard, and unrelenting. He shoves me face-first into the table, pressing me against the wood, and gives me the ride of my life.

The noises that leave me let everyone know what's happening inside Church, and isn't that just sinful?

I love it.

"I'm going to come, Doll. And you. Will. Take. Every. Drop." He punctuates his hips with every word, moaning his pleasure as he comes. I can feel the flex and jerk of his cock, knowing he's orgasming because I made him feel that good.

"Jesse!" I shout his name as one last circle against my clit has me clenching around him, trying to pull him deeper.

He collapses against me, kisses the back of my neck, and we groan when he pulls out. He hurries to slip my panties into place and grabs my shirt while I pull my pants back up. "You do know that everyone probably heard us." He gives a slight pat to my ass, and I shrug my shoulder, uncaring.

I needed that.

I re-hook my bra and pull on my shirt. I fluff my hair and try to look like I wasn't just fucked on the table. "How do I look?"

He grips the edge of the table on either side of me, his taut muscles bulging with the desire to grab me and have his way with me again. "You look like you need my cock again." His hands caress my backside and squeezes. "I don't know what's gotten into you lately, but I fucking love it." He smashes his mouth against me, burying his tongue in my throat and stealing the breath from my lungs as he owns me. He breaks the kiss, and he's right—I'm ready to go another round.

I must be ovulating. I hate that I know my cycle to the nearest second, but I always feel extra rowdy around that time of mouth.

"Now, you need to go to bed, and wait for me naked. When I'm done, I'm going to be inside you—" he blows cold air against my neck, and I whimper "—all night."

The space in front of me loses warmth, and then the door creaks open from his departure. "What the fuck are you looking at? Didn't you say someone is here to see me?" Reaper barks.

"Come and sex! You fucked her good in the pussy!"

A RUTHLESS CHRISTMAS

I hold a hand over my mouth to stifle a laugh.

"Hi, Loch. How are you doing?" Reaper sighs.

"Not as good as you, sex machine, but I bet you have a little dick!"

This is going to be a long night.

Crap.

We didn't get the damn tree.

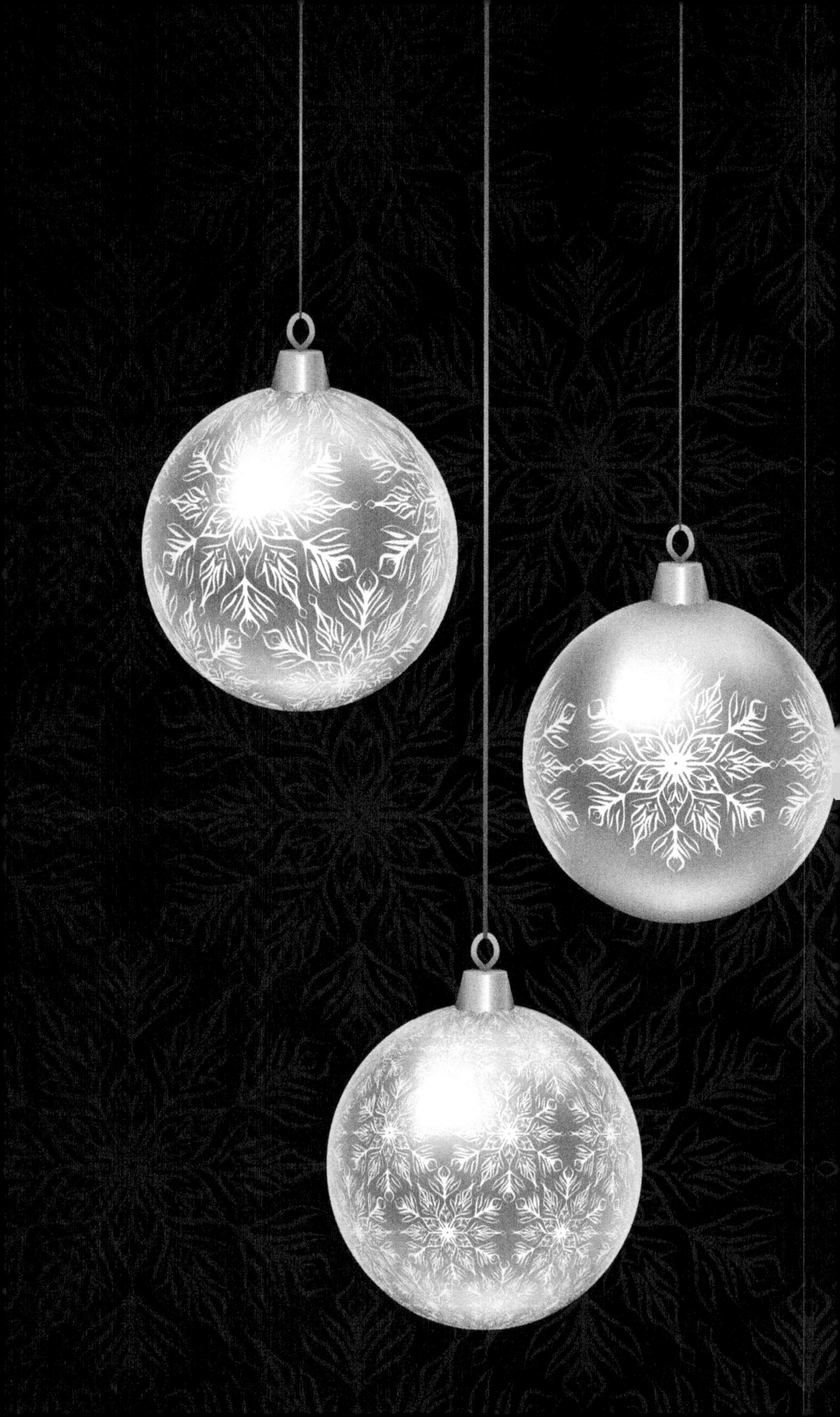

CHAPTER SIX

The Groundskeeper

Look at them. Their festive Christmas spirit makes me sick. There's one hanging up lights right now, wrapping the red, blue, white, green, and yellow lights around the porch. If I remember him correctly, I believe he is the one with the drinking problem.

Maybe it's time I plan my next attack.

If I leave him alone in a room with a shot of whiskey or any alcohol, how long would it take for him to break? A grin stretches my lips as I think about him relapsing. He seems so happy, but I'd bet anything he craves for a drink to slide down his throat even still.

I watch him from the distance with my binoculars as he gets tangled in the lights. They wrap around his legs, and he nearly trips and falls when he pulls tight. Damn, he catches himself.

The tree branch sways from the wind, and I grasp onto it

tightly so I don't fall. The Kings think they can beat me with these walls to keep me out? I will always find a way to hurt them, to try to make them weak. They might have beaten me these few times, but someone will fall.

And all of them will break.

"What are you doing?"

"Shit!" I slip off the branch, and the binoculars fall the ground. The lenses cracks, and anger boils because I know they are ruined. It's my third pair.

The bark scratches against my fingers as I look down to see Zain, the leader of our little misfit loony bin we have created; only I'm not crazy. I know what the hell needs to happen in this world to make it better, and biker scum—along with prostitutes and drug dealers—do not make it a better place. I'm cleaning the place up. People should be thanking me!

I'm not fucking crazy.

"Zain, what are you doing here?"

He crosses his huge arms over his chest. "It's good to see you too, Porter."

"Don't call me that," I seethe. I hate my name.

He rolls his eyes. "The Groundskeeper. That's ridiculous. I'm not calling you that." He rubs a hand over his bald head, then drags it down his face. "Also, I need you to lay off the Ruthless Kings. Okay?"

I let go of the branch and hit the ground. My knees soak up the vibrations as I straighten. "Why?"

"Because no thanks to you and your fucking stupidity, they are our new landlords."

"What? No, that's impossible. I scared them from that place!"

A RUTHLESS CHRISTMAS

"No, you don't scare a King. You only dare them. Plus, I'm related to one."

"You're…" I clench my fists, doing my best not to launch myself at him to wrap my hands around his throat. If he's related to bikers, he's just as bad as they are. Except me. It's not like I asked to be related to Tongue. He's my half-brother.

That doesn't even count.

Plus, I haven't told anyone.

"Which one?" I ask.

"Reaper. He's my nephew."

"I'm so sorry." It disgusts me. How did I not know this when we were all in Riverside Mental Institution together before we broke out? If I would have known, I wouldn't have agreed to live with him.

"Why? It's going to be because of me that we have a home. I'm going to introduce myself, pay rent, and then we can move into the old asylum. You should be thankful."

"I'd rather live on the side of the road than live in a building they own," I spit.

"Then have fun dodging cars, fucker." He flicks me off as he walks away.

"Wait, you're doing it now?" I run after him and shove my hands in my pockets. I can't walk to the front door with him considering Daphne knows my face. Sweet little thing. She's got fight in her that I want to see again. I lift my hand to my head and feel the indentation left from the bar she smacked me with. I wasn't expecting such a hard hit from such a small woman.

It's beautiful.

"Um, yeah, I have to do it now if we want a place to sleep

tonight. The others want a home too, Porter. Not everything is about you." His chest rises and falls, then he snaps his neck from left to right, an audible pop telling me to tread lightly.

I hate treading lightly.

But Zain has this disorder called mania, and when he's in one of his episodes, I know he could kill me if he wanted. A part of me wants to see him try. His mania is triggered when he feels like he has to prove himself. He gets a surge of energy and lashes out, becoming out of focus, desperate, irritable, and he gets an overload of confidence. When he crashes, he enters a depressive episode that can last days, maybe weeks.

Blah, blah, blah. We all have our problems, don't we?

"Stop calling me Porter."

"Realize you have an identity disorder, and maybe I will," he sneers. "Now, go back to the asylum. The others are there." He spins on his cowboy boots and kicks up the desert dust. His lumbering body turns the edge of the wall, and I don't tell him I'm not going back to the asylum. I'm going to watch this unfold.

I grab my broken binoculars from the ground, accidentally getting sand embedded underneath my nails, and climb up the tree again. I lay across the branch like a panther and get into position. "Yes," I cheer when I see only the left lens is broken.

The right is crystal clear.

I peep through the lens and watch Zain get to the front gate. Immediately, a scrawny guy appears from the gate, holding a gun at his head. The guy is brave; I'll give him that. Zain is holding on to the last ounce of strength he has not to release the mania building up inside him. I swing the binoculars

A RUTHLESS CHRISTMAS

to the right and see Reaper standing on the porch. He passes a tangled-up Patrick on his way down the steps to confront Zain.

Oh, this is going to be good; only, someone on the porch has me backtracking, and my breath catches when I see the most beautiful woman I've ever seen. She's helping Patrick untangle himself, laughing at him because he was dumb enough to get twisted up in Christmas lights. Her blonde hair hangs over her shoulders, and her body has parts of me awakening that rubs against the tree branch.

This must be Sarah, Reaper's ol' lady. Isn't that what the bikers call their bitches?

I want her to be mine.

"What a vision," I whisper with awe, just as she bends over to help pick up the lights off the porch. Her ass is fucking perfect. I rock against the tree branch, needing some type of friction as I watch her every move.

I knew she was beautiful. I really did, but my god, I'm seeing her in a new light since the last time I paid a visit here without any of them knowing. She isn't like Daphne. I was only trying to help Daphne when I kidnapped her because we are so much alike. People should stay with their kind of people, you know?

But Sarah might be the exception.

Merry Christmas to me. It looks like I've been a better boy than I thought this year.

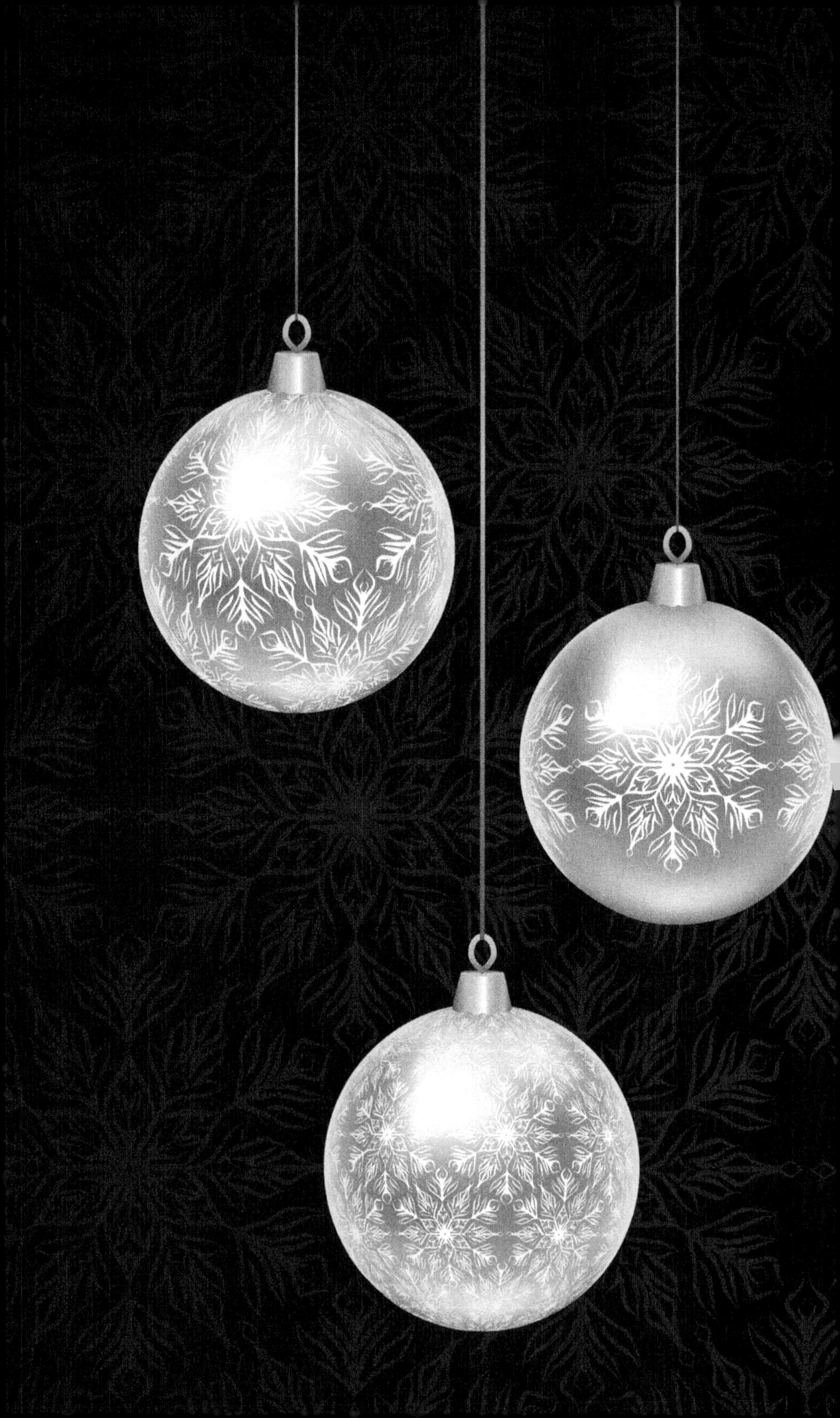

CHAPTER SEVEN

Slingshot

So much happened last night. I thought Reaper's head was going to pop off his body and explode. Not only did we find out his dad got a club whore pregnant, but that he has a sister! A hot sister. Not that I'd ever do anything about the fact that I find her hot. I like that my heart beats in my chest and not Reaper's palm.

So besides that madness, he finds out he has an uncle named Zain, a man he's never met, who was his dad's brother.

Damn, Reaper's getting hit left and right with all the surprises for Christmas.

All I want for Christmas is tacos.

Preferably an all-you-can-eat taco buffet.

I'm not picky, but if I know the guys, they aren't going to get me tacos.

A guy can dream.

There's officially five days left until Christmas, and

while there are decorations everywhere, there's still no tree. My little Miss Avocado is bummed about it. I'm sitting at the kitchen table, waiting to see if Reaper has a brother that's about to walk through the door to stir the pot. I sip my coffee and see Maizey swirl her fork around in her scrambled eggs. It's more like ketchup with eggs, but to each their own, I guess.

It looks disgusting.

She lets out a big dramatic sigh, waiting for me to say something.

I grin around the rim of my mug and nod at Knives when he walks into the kitchen and heads for the coffee pot. His hair is a mess, and he seems like he's still asleep since I can't see his eyes. The man has gotten so many tattoos lately that he hardly looks like the same guy. My favorite one he has is simple. It says 'Judge Me' right where his neck meets his chest.

Maizey lets out another long exhale and taps her fork against the plate, creating that awful fucking sound I hate, so I give in. "What's got your unicorns lacking color, squirt?" I ask her, hating to see her so down.

She sits up and shrugs her tiny shoulders.

"Oh, no, come on. Tell ol' Uncle Slingshot what's wrong." I steal a piece of toast off her plate and bite into it.

"We don't have a tree, and if we don't have a tree, Santa won't come and make my Christmas wishes come true."

"You mean leave presents?" I question.

"No!" she shakes her head, and her dark brown frizzy hair poufs around her shoulders. "If we don't have a tree, then Santa won't know to give Mommy and Daddy a baby.

A RUTHLESS CHRISTMAS

They really want one. I wrote Santa about it and everything, but he hasn't answered. It's because we don't have a tree." Her bottom lip starts to wiggle, and those damn brown eyes get big, but I know what she's doing.

Nope. It isn't going to work. "The puppy eyes aren't going to work on me." I find myself saying that every time because when it comes to Maizey, I seem to be the one to give in the quickest.

Knives snorts, then pretends to clear his throat.

Ass.

"Did you really write Santa a letter for Sarah and Reaper?" My heart melts at the thought. What a sweet kid. And she's calling them Mom and Dad? They must be over the moon.

She nods like a bobblehead. "I did. I did. I even made a copy. Want to see?"

"You made a copy?" Knives repeats her question. His voice is rough with sleep still, tinged with gravel and morning time.

"Just in case Santa didn't get it, duh," she sasses, then leans in and whispers, blocking Knives from reading her lips by placing her hand next to her mouth. "Does he know anything?"

"'Fraid not. Poor guy. He still counts on his fingers."

"Everyone counts on their fingers, Slingshot! If not, you're a liar." He slams his mug down on the table, then picks it back up and stomps out of the room.

"He is so not a morning person," Maizey grins, pinching her lips before scooping up some ketchup egg soup.

Bleh, gross.

"He really isn't." I lean back in the chair until it's balancing on its hind legs, then rock forward. "Okay, I'm not going to be the reason why my Prez and his ol' lady don't get their baby. You want to go get a tree today?"

"Sucker," Badge's voice booms from the back room where he hides away.

"Officer Butthead," Maizey grumbles, then giggles. "I said a bad word."

"I'll let it slide because he is a butthead," I shout the last word over my shoulder to make sure he hears it.

"Okay, go change. We're getting a tree."

"Really?" she squeals.

I point to her breakfast. "After you finish that mess you call food."

She bounces in her chair as she scoops the food into her mouth. Reaper and Sarah walk through the entryway. Neither of them look like they have gotten much sleep with the dark circles around their eyes. "What's all the excitement about, Maze?" Reaper bends down and gives her a quick kiss on top of her head, followed by Sarah.

"Uncle Slingshot is going to take me to get a tree!"

"I want to take her to get a tree." Reaper narrows his eyes at me, pissed that I'd dare take this opportunity away from him.

Oh my God. I can feel him about to take my heart.

I gulp. "I was going to ask before we left."

"We can go together. And we're going to get the biggest tree. Everyone is going!" Reaper announces throughout the house. "Be ready in fifteen." Reaper pours himself some coffee in a white mug that says, 'President of the Unites

A RUTHLESS CHRISTMAS

States of Ruthless America,' a mug I got him as a joke last Christmas. Not to toot my own horn, but he uses it every morning, so…

Toot-toot.

"I'm going to get us the biggest damn tree there is," he grumbles.

"I know you are, baby." Sarah soothes him by rubbing his shoulder.

"Stupid trees. You know, I could go out and chop one down and bring it in here. I'll cut a hole in the roof if I have to."

"I know you would, baby." She continues to be supportive while he vents.

Maizey giggles, and it always makes me laugh because she's so infectious.

"Don't laugh. I'm serious. The biggest tree."

"I know, Daddy," Maizey says with ketchup around her mouth.

"Any tree you want, Maze. You pick, it's yours. Nothing is going to stop me from getting this damn thing!" he bellows, then marches down the hallway and opens his office door. "The biggest fucking tree, got it? We leave in ten minutes, and for the ones who don't show, I'll have you acting like Santa Clause for the next three years!" He slams the door so hard the floor shakes.

"Mommy, Daddy said a bad word."

Sarah gasps and drops the mug she has in her hands, shattering on the floor. Hot coffee and ceramic pieces fly everywhere, but I'm up and out of my seat to get Sarah out of the way.

"Are you okay? Are you hurt?" I ask, just as the office door slams again.

"Doll? What happened?" Reaper says from behind me. "Are you hurt?" Reaper echoes my question and runs to her side, swinging her into his arms, but she fights him.

"I'm fine; put me down. Maze called me Mommy, and it's the first time I heard it." Sarah runs around the other side of the table where it's coffee and mug free, then kneels. "You sure, Maizey? Is that what you want?"

Maizey nods. "Is that okay?"

"Yeah…" She chokes and pulls Maizey in for a hug. "It's more than okay. I'm so happy to be your mommy."

Reaper makes his way over to his family, and I decide this is a good moment to give them some privacy. They've been wanting a child for a long time. We found the families of most of the other kids who were rescued. And it took a while longer to get two more of them back to their families because they were from Mexico. Now all that's left is Maizey and two more who haven't found their homes. They aren't like Maizey, though. They didn't bounce back from being kidnapped. Hell, I forget they are here half the time because I never see them. They stay in a room downstairs. We don't want to put them in foster care, but what do we do? They're too scared to be here.

They should be where they want to be.

I knock on Tongue's door since it's the closest room to escape to and try the knob. I open it and allow myself in, taking a deep breath of relief to be away from the special moment.

"Hi, Slingshot."

A RUTHLESS CHRISTMAS

Tongue's voice startles me, which it shouldn't because it's his room.

My eyes land on the bed, and Daphne is reading while Tongue is placing a Santa hat on his baby gator, Happy. What blows my mind is how Happy is allowing this to happen. "Did you make Happy a Santa hat, Tongue?" I ask, taking a step closer to see if what I'm seeing is real.

"Ain't he cute?" Tongue says with a big smile on his face as he holds up his gator like a proud momma.

The gator opens his mouth wide, and I swear, Happy smiles at me. And damn it, if somehow that reptile doesn't look adorable with that Santa hat on. "He looks very cute, Tongue."

"Oh, that's not all."

It never is when it comes to Tongue.

"Look!" Tongue pulls out a wide red leather collar that has Happy engraved on it in gold. "I got him a matching leash too. For walks."

"Because gators walk. Obviously," I note. Daphne winks at me.

She knows.

"Well, are you going to bring him to get the Christmas tree?" I ask, sitting on the edge of the bed. I reach for Happy to pet the top of his head, but he hisses at me.

"Sorry; he only likes us," Daphne says, patting me on the shoulder before going back to reading her book.

"That's not true." Tongue strokes the spine of his 'swamp kitty' as he calls it. He's such an interesting person. "He likes Patrick and Poodle."

"He almost bit Patrick's finger off," Daphne says, licking

her fingers and flipping the page of the book she's reading. Now that I'm looking around their room for the first time, it's exactly the same as it was before Daphne moved in, only there are books everywhere. In every corner, on top of the dresser, beside the bed, stacked behind the bed to create a headboard. Tongue is the happiest I've ever seen him.

"Patrick insulted him. Happy was defending himself. Isn't that right, good boy?" Tongue scratches under Happy's chin, and the gator shows his teeth and closes his eyes, nearly purring with contentedness.

What the fuck kind of twilight zone is this?

"Let's go! We're getting that damn tree, now!" Reaper bellows.

"Oh, hold on; I need to get his emotional support vest."

I freeze mid-stand. I know I did not hear what I think I just heard. A gator is not an emotional support animal. That can't even be legal.

The proof is right there before my eyes, though. He slips the vest over Happy's body, and on the side in white block letters it reads, 'Emotional support animal in training.'

"Oh, such a good boy, Happy." Tongue places Happy on the ground and reaches into a red jar, pulling out pink chunks of... something. He tosses the treat in the air, and Happy's jaws smack together.

I have a feeling those were bite-sized pieces of tongue.

And he keeps them in a Mason jar.

Next to his bed.

I need to get out of here.

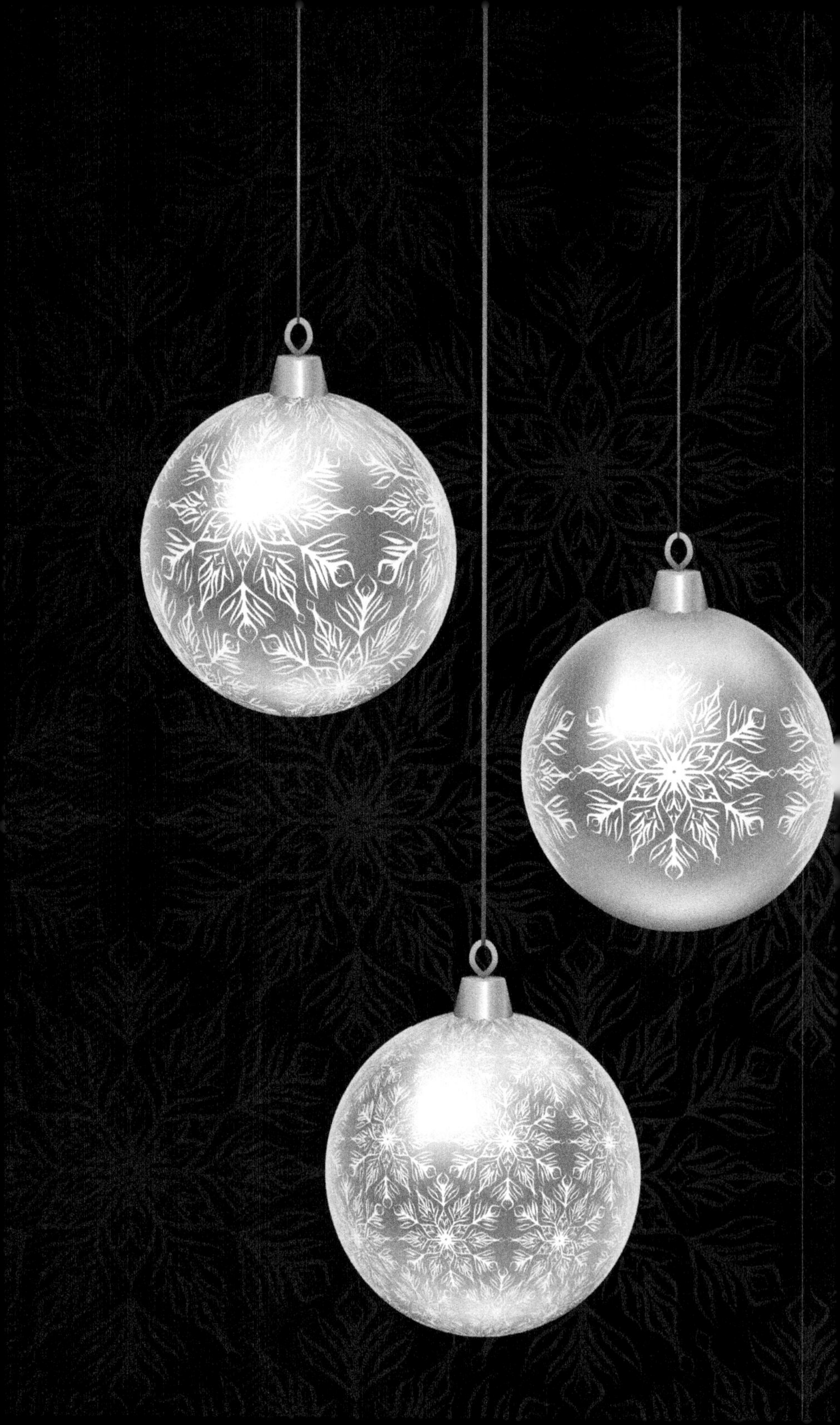

CHAPTER EIGHT

Poodle

"WHAT DO YOU MEAN, CANCER? I DON'T UNDERSTAND," I say to the vet, stroking Lady's side as she pants. My heart is hammering in my chest. "She's only been tired, maybe a little lethargic. I got her new food; maybe it's that?"

"James, she's extremely sick. It isn't the food. It's bone cancer."

"No," I frown, shaking my head. "It isn't bone cancer. She's fine. I only changed her food."

"Have you noticed that she isn't moving around as much? Not eating as much?"

"She's older; that's all," I whisper, my vision blurring with sudden heat. "She's old," I repeat, then envelope my best friend in my arms. I bury my nose in her fluffy fur and squeeze my eyes shut.

Melissa's hand lands on top of mine, sliding through

Lady's fur to bring me comfort. I don't think anything could ever bring me comfort.

"I know this is a hard decision and not the right time, but I suggest putting her to sleep. The longer you wait, the more pain she will be in. Her cancer has spread to her kidneys and lungs."

"I'm not putting her to sleep. I can't. No!" I yell at Dr. Adamson, the woman who has been Lady's vet since she was just a pup. "I can't. Not right now." A tear falls from my eye. I don't even care who sees me in my cut, crying over my dog.

She isn't just my dog. She's my family.

"This cannot be real. She had puppies late in life. Was that the reason she's sick?"

"No, that's not the reason, James. She's old. That's all. Her health is declining. This is the day we have both feared ever since you got her as a puppy."

"But I didn't think the end would come so fast," I say, and Lady lifts her head up, giving me kisses along my palm. "Not before Christmas."

"We can wait until after Christmas, but, James, if you wait any longer, you'll be prolonging a massive amount of pain. I'll make sure to send home pain killers too."

"I should have brought her in earlier." I wipe my cheek on my sleeve. "When she started getting so tired. I should have known, but I didn't. I just thought she was getting old, and it was normal. I could have saved her."

"No, you can't think like that," Dr. Adamson tells me softly. "Even if you had brought her in sooner, her age wouldn't have given her a good chance."

"Such a good girl, Lady." I scratch the place behind her

ear that she likes so much. "You have been my best friend for so long, and I promise, I'm going to give you the best Christmas of your life." Since she has issues walking, I slide my hands under her and pick her up, cradling her to my chest. Melissa lifts her phone and takes a picture of us and I lean forward, placing a kiss on her lips. She knows I'm going to want all the pictures of me and Lady before she passes away.

I can't even think about it. I'm a strong man. I'm not afraid to admit that I've done awful fucking things that will drag me to Hell. Animals are so much better than people in my opinion. People are assholes, but animals are loyal no matter what. The human race is vile, and we sure as hell don't deserve something as pure as an animal's love.

"Dad?" Ellie, my daughter, whispers my name outside the door as I walk through it. Ellie didn't want to be in the exam room because she said all she'd do is cry, but looking at her face, it seems that's all she's been doing anyway. "What did the vet say?"

"I'll tell you in the truck," I say, burying Lady's head in my shoulder as we stroll down the beige hallway toward the front door. The walls are lined with Christmas crap, red bows, cotton to mimic snow, and then wish-lists from other animal owners lined throughout.

When I get to the door, I turn around and push it open with my back. The winter air bursts over my heated face. I feel like I'm about to fall over. I hold Lady tighter and lean my weight against the truck, taking a minute to myself.

Melissa and Ellie are about to come outside, and I need to be strong for them, even if I'm falling apart on the inside. "Lady, I love you. I need you to know that, okay?"

She whines and licks my cheek. I know she can understand me. We've spent too much time together over the years. She knows what love feels like, and that makes me so happy that I gave her a good life. I want more. I expected her to live forever, which is ridiculous, but it's the truth.

"Dad, what did the vet say?" Ellie asks as soon as she opens the door. God, every time I look at her, my heart hurts just a little because I see the shadow of her mother.

Do I lie to her? I can't. I need to prepare her too. It wouldn't be fair. "She has cancer, Ellie. After Christmas we have to say goodbye."

"What! No," Ellie cries. "It's Lady. Lady can't... No! The vet is wrong."

Ah, she might look like her mother, but her denial is all me, isn't it?

"I wish she was, baby, but Lady is old, and it's showing."

Melissa comes through the door last, and the mascara under her eyes is smudged from crying too. It feels like I'm losing a child. Lady is everything to me. Especially before Melissa and Ellie came into my life. What the hell am I going to do?

"Um..." Melissa wipes under her eyes. "Reaper messaged and said everyone is going to get a Christmas tree. Do you want to meet them or go home? I'm sure he'll understand if we don't meet them there."

"No, we should go. It's Lady's last Christmas. She deserves to see everything." It breaks my heart that this will be the last time she experiences it. I open the door to the truck and gently place Lady in her dog seat and buckle her in. Another tear falls as her cold nose presses against my cheek,

A RUTHLESS CHRISTMAS

and a whimper escapes her when she senses my sadness. I reach up and scratch her neck, then kiss her snout. "Best fucking dog in the world, Lady. Best fucking dog." I shut her door, and I'm immediately engulfed in a hug from Ellie.

I wrap my arms tight around Ellie. She hasn't been in my life long because I thought she died when she was a baby. I don't know what I'd do without her. My life is rich with her and Melissa in it. I'm a wealthy man, and it isn't because of money.

It's because of love.

The one thing my old self never would have thought I'd have.

"Are you okay?" Melissa asks me as Ellie lets go of me and climbs in the passenger seat.

"No," I answer honestly. I grab the passenger door and close it behind Ellie. I need to get out of this parking lot. "I know Lady is just a dog—"

Melissa places her finger over my mouth, and the waves of her dark hair flow over her shoulders. She recently got bangs, which was an accident because she got bored one night, but I fucking love them. They frame her face and make her emerald eyes seem brighter. She stands on her tiptoes and places a soft kiss against on my lips. "She isn't just a dog. She's never been just a dog. You don't have to explain your heartache because I feel it too. She's our family, James. She was there for me during the worst time of my life and brought me comfort. She helped find Dawn; she has saved so many of us. She deserves peace."

My forehead falls on Melissa's, her skin surprisingly warm with how cold it is outside. Even in winter, she smells like a summer's day. "Let's go get that tree. I'm sure Reaper is ready to chop a cactus down at this point because we've waited so long." I want to change the subject. I don't want to talk about Lady anymore. I don't want to dwell on the fact that in five days, I'm going to lose my oldest friend.

It's Christmastime.

We deserve to feel happiness, and so does Lady. She isn't dead yet, and we aren't going to act like she is. I take Melissa's chin in my hand and place another kiss against her lips before we walk hand-in-hand around the truck. I open the back door for her, and she slides next to Lady, buckling herself in, then petting our loyal guardian.

Nope, can't do it. I won't fucking cry.

I'll let go when she closes her eyes one last time.

Telling myself that, my eyes dry up, and I compartmentalize my emotions so I can make it through the next week. I click the seatbelt over my chest, check to make sure everyone I love is safe and secure too, and check the mirrors. My eyes meet Melissa's, the love of my damn life, and I put the truck in reverse.

The further away I get from the vet's office, the better. We get on Loneliest Road, and drive past the exit we would take to go to the strip. About ten minutes later, we're in front of a pop-up Christmas tree sale.

And it doesn't look promising.

A line of bikes is parked along with a few trucks to hold the bigger families of the club, like Reaper and Sarah who have Maizey.

"Oh, no," I say when I see Tongue standing there with his gator in a baby sling on his chest. It's the most ridiculous thing I've ever seen. I pound my forehead against the wheel and Melissa starts to giggle, along with Ellie when they see Tongue. "Well, I guess I can't get too close to Tongue or Happy will attack Lady, and we can't have that."

Lady barks twice in agreement.

"I know, right?" I tell her, opening the truck door and jumping out into the cold desert night.

"What the fuck do you mean you don't have any eight-foot trees? Give me a ten-foot tree then," Reaper bellows, and the baritone of his voice bounces off the mountain.

"Someone is going to die tonight," Ellie singsongs.

"Ellie!" Melissa scolds.

"She isn't wrong, Sunflower," I snort, opening the back door to get Lady. I gather her in my arms and then hold her like I would Melissa. I wrap her back legs around my waist and put her front paws on my shoulder. "Good girl."

Lady lays her chin on my shoulder, her energy drained. She's exhausted.

My baby.

Melissa, Ellie, Lady, and I walk toward our big, weird, crazy family. Dawn is next to Skirt, cuddled against him with her hair in some sort of knot on top of her head while Skirt rocks the stroller back and forth. Aidan is hooked to Dawn's leg, who is actually Skirt's nephew; that was a shocker. They make a beautiful family too. I'm happy for the fighter.

There is Tool and Juliette, who are completely night and day. As far as I know, kids aren't in the plan yet just like with Patrick and Sunnie; they aren't ready yet.

Then there is Tongue and Daphne.

There are no words to explain how they work. Tongue

is as dark as the horror stories people warn their kids about, and Daphne is the innocent book nerd who wears glasses. Yet, I'm watching them, and she has her head leaned against his shoulder, and she pecks the tip of Happy's snout.

Who. Kisses. A. Gator?

A crazy person.

"I don't give a fuck if your men have to go out and chop down my tree. You're going to do it."

Hearing Reaper get heated yanks me from my judgy thoughts, and I watch the scene unfold. There is one tree left, and it's dead. It's nothing but twigs. One good gust of wind and that thing is going to blow to pathetic pieces.

"How much are you willing to pay?" The salesmen smirks.

Oh, he has no idea who the hell he's talking to.

Right before Reaper can say anything, Maizey stands in front of her dad and pushes the salesman. "Listen, I have an uncle who will cut your tongue out and feed it to his kitty, so you better pay up!"

Her childish, high-pitched voice is adorable when she tries to sound threatening. She's so little, but she's sassy. I feel bad for Reaper when she becomes a teenager. She's going to be impossible to argue with.

"Is that right?" The salesman leers as he grins his nasty yellow teeth at her, then scratches his crotch. Reaper reaches behind him and pulls out the knife he always keeps on him, but Tongue beats him to it.

"Oh, the princess is spot on." Tongue's ghoulish tone matches the evil intent shining against the black tungsten of his knife as he holds it against the man's neck. He tilts his

A RUTHLESS CHRISTMAS

head, and Happy tilts his too, then opens his mouth and lets out a hiss. "The kitty she talks about is a gator, and he loves a good tongue. I should cut yours out for how you just talked to Maizey."

Tongue's arm has finally regained some motion again after being shot, but he isn't listening to Doc. It isn't going to heal, and he might not ever get full motion if he doesn't stop pushing himself. Only time will tell, but it doesn't look too promising.

"Let him have it, Tongue!"

"Maizey," Sarah says her name in a way that tells her to hush and be quiet. Sarah steps in front of Maizey to protect her from the man.

The man starts to sweat, and I glance down at his nametag and roll my eyes when I see that his name is Frank. I feel like all assholes are named Frank for some reason.

"Let's go for a walk. I want a tree for my princess. I want it now. If you're lucky I won't filet you like a fish and feed you to Happy."

The smell of piss fills the air, and Tongue smirks while the stench wakes the baby, causing Joey to cry.

"I love the smell of fear." Tongue buries his nose in the back of the man's head and trembles, as if he's turned on.

Curious, I glance toward Daphne, who's biting her lips as she checks Tongue out while he sniffs the tree salesman.

How did men like us end up with perfect partners?

Christmas miracle.

If only that applied to my Lady.

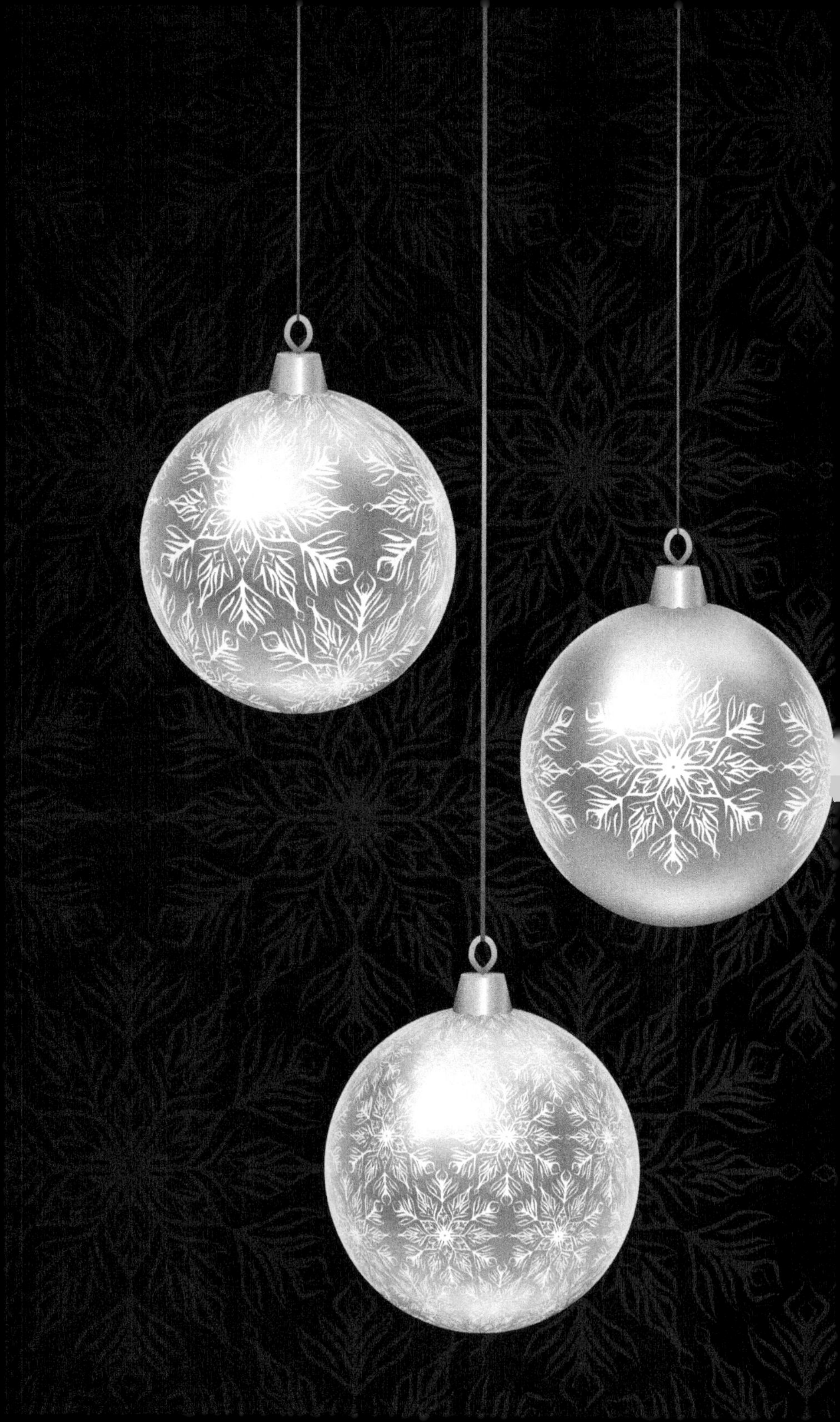

CHAPTER NINE

Sarah

"I can't believe we're decorating a cactus." I giggle while Doc plucks needles out of Reaper's arm. He really did go chop down the biggest tree he could find, but he only found a cactus. The guys are around the cactus, wearing gloves and plucking the needles out one by one so no one hurts themselves. We will leave a few needles up top for decorations, but the bottom will be bare.

And it's taking so long.

"Well, if Tongue hadn't been so quick to kill the salesman, maybe we wouldn't be here right now. Ow, Doc!" Reaper jerks his arm back, and Doc rolls his eyes. There has to be a hundred different pinpricks along his arms beading blood.

"You survived an explosion, Reaper. You can deal," Doc says dryly, plucking another needle from his arm.

"Well, if I didn't have to put the Harley Davidson star on

the cactus, by myself, I wouldn't have had so many needles. Ow! Doc, Jesus. Don't pluck my fucking arm off."

No one would put the Harley Davidson star on the cactus because of all the sharp pinpoints sticking out all over the place and Reaper was a few inches too short to miss a few needles. He will be okay. He's just cranky.

The tree topper is cute. When it plugs into the wall, a white light shines from it and a cut out piece of metal that says Harley Davidson is across the front. The light shines through the cutout letters in the metal and casts them on the wall.

"You. Survived. An. Explosion," Doc punctuates every word, taking his tweezers and yanking another needle out.

"Yes, Reaper. You survived an explosion. Hurray," Moretti fake cheers, then plucks a needle from the cactus and purposely stabs Bullseye in the arm.

"What the fuck, Moretti!" Bullseye bellows.

"Don't you need to check your blood sugar?" Moretti says matter-of-factly.

"I don't need to check it! I'm fine."

"Is that why you aren't waking up until the day is nearly over?"

Color me shocked, but it sounds like Moretti cares. We've all been worried about Bullseye's denial about his type-2 diabetes. It's serious. He needs insulin, but he's living like nothing ever happened. No matter how many times Doc tells him, or we plead our concerns for his health, nothing we say gets through his head.

"I'm tired. I've been going on long runs for Reaper; everyone knows that."

A RUTHLESS CHRISTMAS

"You haven't enjoyed your fun with your favorite couple. That's a big deal. Don't you have a weekly meeting with them?"

I gasp, hanging a candy cane on one of the needles. Moretti might have just signed his death warrant. Everyone knows what Skirt, Bullseye, and Dawn do together. Granted, not much has happened since she's had the baby because she can't have sex yet, but it's only a matter of time. No one talks about it. It isn't our business. They are happy, and that's all that matters.

"What the fuck did ye just say?" Skirt comes around from the other side of the Christmas cactus, clenching his scarred fists in preparation for a fight. "Yer going to want to make sure of what ye say next or I'll make sure ye don't breathe again."

"Like that scares me," Moretti rolls his eyes, unimpressed with Skirt's threat as he hangs a sleigh ornament on the cactus. "I'm pointing out facts. It isn't a secret what you three do behind closed doors. Hell, I don't care." He laughs gently, placing his hand against his chest. "I wish I could join. I can't remember what I like, but I have a feeling I'd like that. I think I love a man in a kilt. Everyone here is tiptoeing around Bullseye because of his diabetes, yet no one is holding him accountable. Don't you think it's time he isn't treated like a baby?"

Skirt punches Moretti before any of us can blink again. I move out of the way before Moretti falls against me. Reaper wraps his arm around me, pulling me to his side for safety. If I had to bet who would win this fight, it would be Skirt. He's a professional fighter and blood thirsty. Skirt raises his fist again, and my eyes land on his knuckles. The living room light shines against the red wetness splattering across his fingers from Moretti's busted lip.

Blood has never bothered me.

But it does today.

I yank myself out of Reaper's arms and run to the closest bathroom. It's the one Poodle uses, and the lavender scent from his shampoo is everywhere, which usually smells good, but not this time. It heightens my gag reflex, and I barely have time to lift the lid and puke. Then the smell of the bathroom just makes it worse. That ... toilet water smell slams into my nostrils and I throw up again.

"Doll! Damn it, what's wrong? Are you okay?" Reaper's hand lands in the middle of my back, and the heat radiating from him feels good.

"I'm sorry, Sarah. I didn't mean to make you sick," Moretti says over Reaper's shoulder, next to Skirt.

Are they friends now? Did they just need a good scuffle? I don't understand men.

"Doll, what's wrong? Talk to me," Reaper rubs soothing circles between my shoulder blades, and it helps with the nausea.

"I don't know. I saw the blood on Skirt's knuckles." I gag again, not wanting to talk about it. "Then the bathroom smells terrible."

"It smells like my shampoo. That does not smell terrible," Poodle defends.

"Well, it does to me!" Another spasm twists my stomach, and I shoo everyone away with my hand. "Please, go away. This isn't a show." All I want to do is decorate the Christmas

A RUTHLESS CHRISTMAS

cactus. Is it perfect? No, but it seems pretty fitting considering we're all imperfect. I think the cactus needs to be a tradition in the Ruthless household.

I hear a hiss, and I lift my head from the toilet to see Tongue standing there, Happy strapped to his chest, and there's red along Happy's sharp teeth.

The tree salesman.

Oh, I'm going to throw up again.

"Here, take him." He lifts Happy from the sling and hands him over to Poodle, who holds him out like Badge did to Maizey last night.

"Uh," Poodle says cautiously as Happy hisses.

Tongue squats on the other side of me and flushes the toilet, tears off a few sheets of TP, and wipes my mouth. "Do you think you could be pregnant?" Tongue asks.

"Yes! Hell yes, she can!" Reaper announces with a clap of his hands. "You hear that, Doll? You're pregnant."

"We don't know that," I say, slowly lifting myself off the floor. I want to go lay down.

"You're sick. Smells are bothering you. It makes sense." Reaper's hand lands on my arm, and I shrug him off.

I'm getting angry. "I'm not pregnant! I'm just sick. God, just stop! Everyone just stop. It hasn't happened. It won't happen, and giving me hope is just fucking cruel! Let it go, Reaper. Everyone just..." I cover my face with my hands and catch a sob. "Just stop, please. Just stop."

I run between the members who crowded outside the bathroom and head toward the room we've been staying in. I slam the door, then lock it for good measure. I need to be alone. I need time to think.

I flip on the fan to help with the sweat building on my skin and throw myself on the bed. I grab Reaper's pillow and hug it to my chest. Slow, painful sobs shake my body, and I can hardly breathe. I want to be pregnant.

I don't want to be pregnant.

I'm scared.

"Sarah?" Doc calls out my name from behind the door. Right now it's muted and soft, but I know once the door opens, it will be loud and reassuring.

I can't handle that right now.

I don't answer him. I inhale Reaper's scent and let myself get lost in the comfort he brings me. If I am pregnant, what then? Doc told me once a woman has one miscarriage, it's probable she will have another. I can't go through that again.

"Sarah? Open the door, Doll."

I feel awful for acting this way. After all the trying, we might finally have what we want, and I'm terrified. I don't want them to give me hope. I don't want to talk about me being pregnant because if I'm not, I'll be crushed.

If I am, I'll be crushed. What if I can't protect him or her? The safest place for a baby is inside it's mother's womb, and I don't have that ability.

I'll lose it again.

"Sarah, open the door, or I'm going to break it down," Reaper threatens.

"Go away," I say, burying my face in the pillow.

I hear his deep sigh on the other side of the door, and the wood creaks, probably from him leaning against it. "Never, Doll. I'm never going anywhere. Open up this door and talk to me. Talk to Doc. I know you're scared, but I'm here. You know I'm going to fight every ounce of your fear like it's my own. Open the door so we can get answers and see what we need to do. Come on, Doll."

"Mommy? What did you do, Daddy?" Maizey accuses him.

"I only did what she wanted me to," Reaper says as innocently as he can, which makes me smile.

He did. I asked for a baby, and now I might have one.

I sit up and wipe the tears off my cheeks, still hugging his pillow. I glance toward the door and sniffle, unsure if I want to go down this road. If I'm pregnant, what steps can we take to make sure I'm able to carry the baby to full term?

Fresh water brimming my eyes, I stand and twist my hands together. When I get to the door, I unlock it without opening it, then hurry back to bed to lay down. I'm not feeling well, and I don't know if it's because of panic or the stomach flu.

The knob turns, and light spills in from the hallway into the dark room. "Sarah, Doll, what's going on?" Reaper sits next me, and the bed dips so low from his weight, I grip the side of the mattress to prevent myself from rolling off. He takes my hand and intertwines our fingers while Maizey climbs up and sits next me, laying her head on my shoulder.

"We got a tree, and Santa brought you a baby just like I asked," Maizey states cheerfully.

"What do you mean?" I ask her.

"I wrote Santa. Told him to give you a baby, but we didn't have a tree, so I knew it wouldn't happen unless we had a tree."

"Oh, Maze." I hold her against me and place my chin on top of her head.

"You don't want this anymore?" Reaper asks, his hope broken, but he holds my hand anyway.

"What? No, that's not it!" I sit up and lay our hands over my belly. "I'm so scared. If I am, I will be equally as happy and terrified. I'll be afraid to move, to breathe, to do anything to risk losing our baby."

"Anything you do won't be the reason why. These things, they just…" He sighs, blinking toward the ceiling as he takes a deep breath and exhales. "They happen."

"He's right, Sarah," Doc sets his medical kit on the floor beside the vintage nightstand I bought from a local antique store. "You can walk, breathe, eat, laugh, but even just laying here can put you at risk for a miscarriage. Let's take a test."

"But the stabbing…"

"I know," Doc says with a grimace twitching his mouth. "I'm not going to bite off more than I can chew right now. The first step is to see if you are pregnant. I'm going to take a blood test; it's quicker and will tell us if your hCG levels are elevated."

"Okay." I nod, holding out my arm for him to wrap the rubber band around my bicep to plump the vein. I squeeze Reaper's arm, holding onto him as if I'm about to drift away. He's my anchor, the strength that keeps me still in the storm that rages around us.

Doc cleans the inside of my elbow, sanitizes it, then draws a few vials of blood. "Okay, I'll get this downstairs right now and test them. You'll know by the end of the day. Everything is going to be okay."

A RUTHLESS CHRISTMAS

Doc gives us a parting smile before exiting the room and closing the door behind him. Joanna is pregnant too, and Skirt and Dawn's daughter Joey is barely a few months old. If I am too, our kids will grow up close in age. How exciting would that be?

"Do you want to come decorate the tree?" Reaper asks.

"We can stay in here if you want."

"No. I want to enjoy the night with my family." Maybe this will be the last Christmas it will be the three of us.

One can only hope.

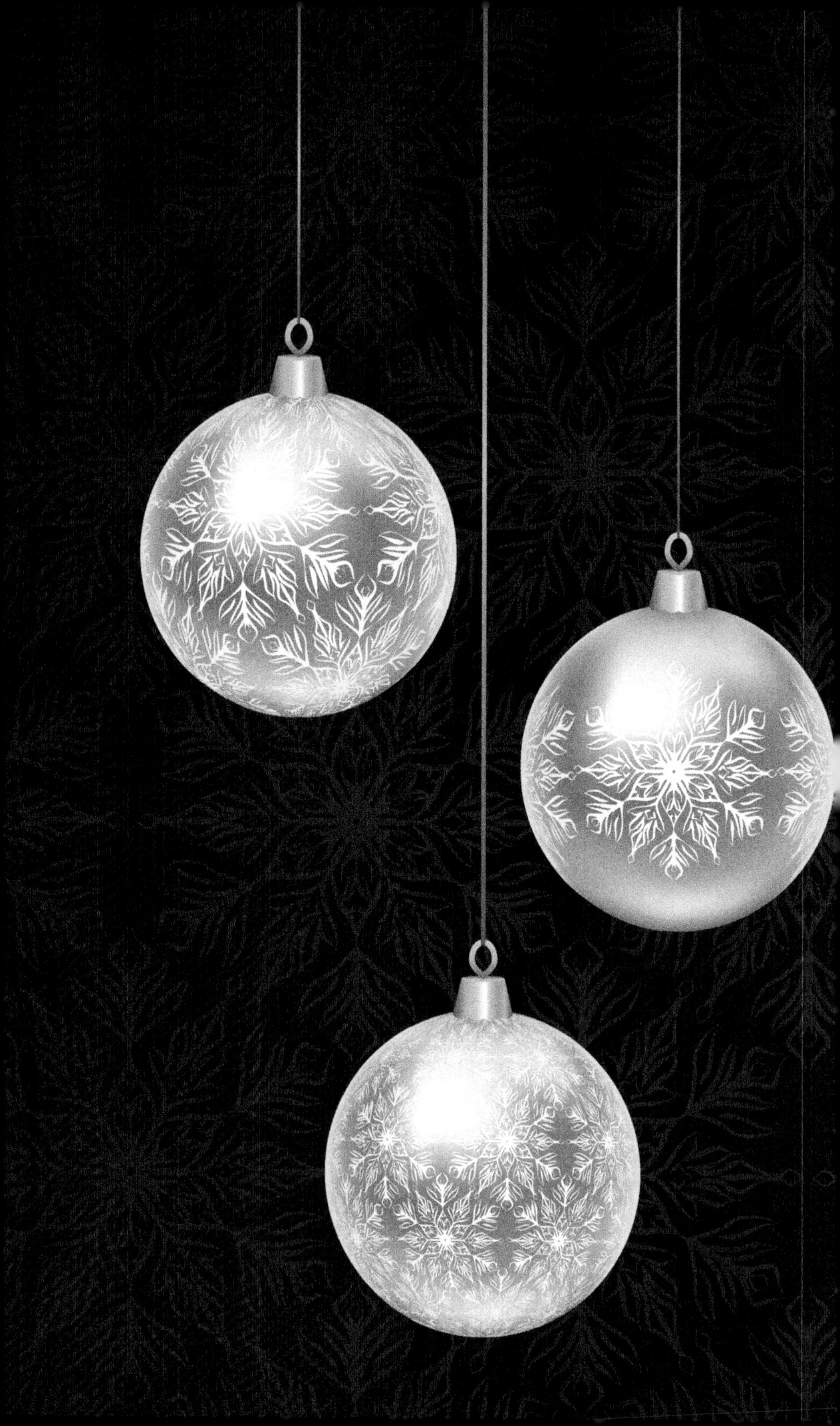

CHAPTER TEN

Tongue

Four days until Christmas.

I got my comet the only thing in the world she's ever wanted.

A bookstore.

Andrew's bookstore, which I know will hold some meaning for her. I don't know why. The guy was a complete waste of space, but just because I can't understand her feelings doesn't mean they aren't valid. I'll love her through them, even if I disagree.

Plus, the bookstore has this really old book she likes, and I want her to have it. I want her to have everything.

I can't wait until Christmas. I got the keys to the place yesterday. The bookstore was supposed to go to next of kin if something happened to Andrew, and since something did happen, I had to threaten the lawyer that I'd kill him and feed him to Happy for that not to happen.

I won, and the lawyer still speaks.

How do I want to surprise her? Women like that, right? She deserves it. She's been teaching me how to read, but since I'm a fucking idiot, it's taking a long time. I'm lucky to read three words before I get frustrated and throw the book across the room.

"Tongue? I need your help. I can't—" Daphne grunts as she stretches her arm to grab a book on the shelf I just installed, "—I can't reach it."

Of course, she can't. What would make her think she could? It's an entire foot above her. Sometimes, I don't understand her efforts. I like watching her try, though. Her ass jiggles every time she loses her balance, and my cock hardens. I growl as her sleek body moves. A body that's mine. I was just inside her this morning, but I want her again.

I can't because there's no time. I need to take her to the bookstore, and then we're going to do some last-minute Christmas shopping for everyone. All I want to do is stay in bed, deep inside her tight cunt, rubbing her body with my knife that I had engraved with her. I want her to beg me to cut her, to carve my name into her chest like she wanted before.

"Wayne," she gasps as I pick her up and throw her on the bed.

Christmas can wait. It isn't like it's going anywhere. It will be there next year, and the year after, and then the year after that. And since me and Daphne are going to be together for all eternity and in death, I think it's safe to say we will have plenty of holidays.

Daphne's tits bounce as she settles on our mattress. Her

A RUTHLESS CHRISTMAS

nipples are hard, tenting the shirt she's wearing. "We have to go shopping. We can't," she moans as I strip off my shirt.

She loves my body for some fucked up reason, but it's why we're meant to be together. She loves me, and only the Devil knows why.

I'm about to unzip my jeans so her plump lips can wrap around my cock and suck me down her throat, when someone who has a death wish knocks on the door. I curl my lips, grab my knife from on top of the dresser, and lick it. I'm ready to kill somebody for interrupting me.

"Be nice," Daphne says with a giggle.

"I am nice," I grouse.

I open the door and place the tip of the blade under the visitor's chin. "Boomer," I greet with zero excitement. Maybe I would've been if he didn't interrupt me. "I didn't know you were coming. You and your members here?" If they are, I'll have to take Daphne away from here. I don't know Boomer's guys like I know the Vegas members. They will want her. I'm not afraid to cut out their tongues. I don't care if they are brothers by the Ruthless name. I'll kill.

I'll bathe in their blood victoriously, and you know what Daphne will do?

She'll join me.

Oh, now that would be the perfect Christmas gift. Maybe we can find someone walking down the strip again and do a little hunting, have some fun, let our hair down.

"It's good to see you too, Tongue. Merry Christmas."

"I would say it's good to see you too, but I'm busy."

He peers around my shoulder, not doubt seeing my

beautiful comet laying in bed. His eyes widen. "Well, how are you doing? I'm Boom—Ow!"

I drop my knife from his chin and slice it across is arm. "Don't." I wave the blade in front of him.

"I should've known that even after you found someone, you'd still be a psychopath."

"Don't call him that!" Daphne comes to my defense and loops her arm through mine. I tilt my head down and notice her glasses are crooked, so I straighten them and push the frames up the bridge of her nose.

Damn, I'm a lucky man.

"Does anyone know you're here? Reaper didn't mention you coming."

"I tried calling him, but he hasn't been answering, so no, I don't think anyone knows we're here. I'm excited to see everyone, meet all the new members we have—"

"We have. Not you. You left, remember?" I didn't know it bothered me that he left until this moment. "Don't say we. You picked a new family."

"Tongue, you're still my family. That hasn't changed. You know why I had to leave."

Daphne's body sinks into mine as she leans against me. She got new shampoo that reminds me of the beach. Coconut and some type of flower. I love it. I concentrate on her, her curves, her scent, the softness of her hair, and breathe out. "Everyone is actually downstairs to see if Sarah is pregnant. Everyone is excited," I finally say.

"Why aren't you?" His misfit market of members come from down the hallway, and the twins look Daphne up and down like she's candy.

A RUTHLESS CHRISTMAS

"Mine," I sneer at them while they bump knuckles.

"Lay off, guys. Daphne is taken, and you do not want to fuck with Tongue, got it?" Boomer says over his shoulder, but he never stops looking me in the eye.

"Got it, Prez." The one that has the name patch 'Warden' on his cut, nods his head and turns into the kitchen across the hall.

Wolf is next to him, a guy I never thought I'd like because of what happened with the Jersey Chapter, but I do. He's a good guy who was trying to save his sister. Arrow, One-Eye, and Kansas drag the chairs out from the table and get comfortable. Wolf seems bored, so he finds the coffee pot instead of standing here and talking to me. He rinses it out and stares out the window. He slushes the water around in the pot, washing out all the flavor.

Doesn't he know that's a cardinal sin?

He tilts his head and pauses what he's doing, almost as if he's lost in thought. The faucet runs, and water flows down the sink, gurgling through the pipes. Wolf releases the handle, and the glass pot breaks in the sink, ruining any chance for coffee.

But he has a reason.

He dashes down the hall, toward the main room, and out the front door, leaving it wide open so the dusty air can get in.

Curious, Boomer and his men head out the door, but I don't follow.

"What the fuck is the racket about, Tongue?" Reaper opens the basement door, which jingles since Maizey put a bell on it. "I'm trying to see if my wife is pregnant."

"Boomer is here," I drawl.

His face lights up like our Christmas Cactus in the living room. "Doc! Wait. Sarah, Boomer is here!"

A high-pitched squeal has my ears ringing.

You know what follows Boomer? Explosions. I want a quiet Christmas. Maybe a little blood, a lot of sex, maybe at the same time, but I do not feel like getting blown up.

"Is there a story I'm missing?" Daphne asks me, tugging on my cut.

I shut the bedroom door and grin. "Oh, yeah."

She jumps on the bed, excited like a teenage girl about to gossip. "Tell me, tell me, tell me," she begs.

I mock her, jumping on the bed too, but my weight breaks it. One side of the mattress falls to the floor when a metal rod snaps, and I grab onto Daphne to make sure she's okay.

But she's laughing so hard she can't breathe. "You … you … can't jump on beds. You're … too big," she gasps, her face turning red.

I'm getting worried. Do I need to breathe for her? Blow into her mouth? I will.

"I was excited to tell you the story."

"Tell me. I'm listening, Comet," she smiles.

Bed broken, books scattered, the remainder of the bed's frame moaning from having to support the weight.

My arm hurts, but I don't care. If I can be here with Daphne, what more could I want for Christmas? I have my swamp kitty, my knives, my tongues, and love. The only thing I need to fix is my relationship with Sarah. Boomer asked why I wasn't excited.

I am.

I just don't think she wants me there when she gets the news.

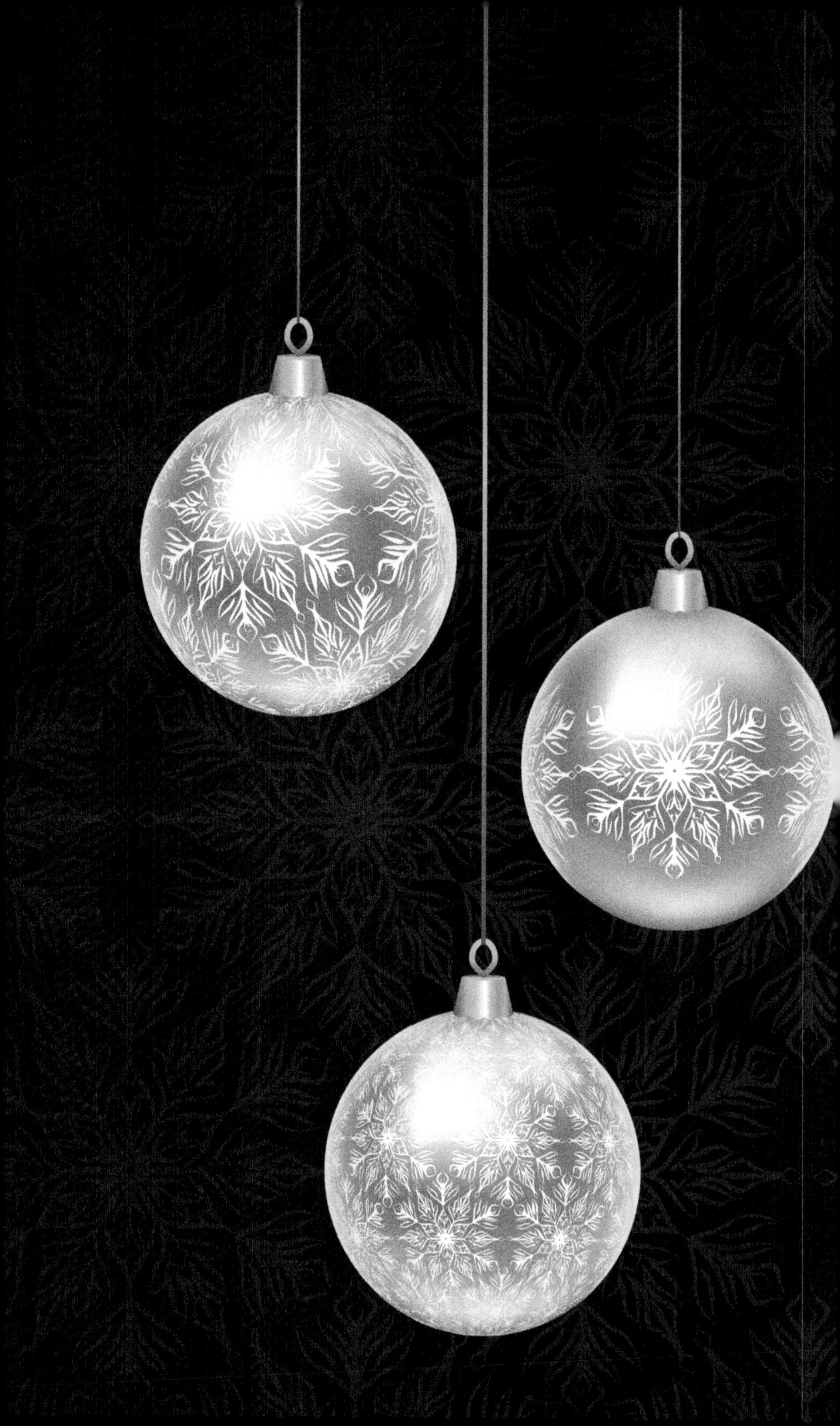

CHAPTER ELEVEN

DOC

Everyone is giving Boomer hugs and pats on the back for his surprise Christmas visit. At this rate, I expect everyone we know to show up, like the NOLA chapter, which I kind of hope happens. I want to see Tool creeped out by Seer.

"Doc, how are you, man?" Boomer comes in for a hug. Damn, I can't believe this is the same brat who used to set trash can fires at school. He's really grown up. His hair is longer, and it looks like he has a few more tattoos. His cut is still blank, but that doesn't seem to matter to the guys who follow him. After what a few members have been through, they're probably relieved to be able to breathe for a minute.

"I'm alright. It's good to see you, Boomer. I'm happy you came. Where's Scarlett?"

"Ah, she stayed back with Homer. He isn't feeling too well lately, and since he's older than dirt, she didn't feel right leaving him alone."

"Scarlett's sweet like that," I say, leaning against the porch beam and casting a glance at Boomer's VP, Wolf, as he traipses around outside. Right as I was about to tell Sarah and Reaper their results, Boomer interrupted us. "What's your boy doing, Boomer?"

"I don't know. He thinks he saw someone up in the tree. He's going to check it out, but he's a paranoid motherfucker. I doubt someone is going to climb up that tree to look over the wall. That's a bit much," Boomer says. He pulls out a flask, and I snag his wrist, stopping him before he can even think about taking a swig of it. "What?" he asks.

"You better put that shit away. Patrick is around. Have some respect."

"Fuck, I can't believe I forgot that. I'm sorry." Boomer tucks the flask in his cut pocket and catches a glimpse of Wolf headed back to us. "I know that look," he says, pushing off the wall with his boot. He jumps off the porch instead of taking the steps.

I know that tone of voice he used, and it isn't a good one.

Not wanting him to walk by himself, I'm at his side, ready to take on the news Wolf is about to deliver. "So is Sarah pregnant? Have you told her?"

"I can't talk about that with you. You know that."

"I know. I hope she is. They deserve it after everything that's happened." Boomer eyes where Skirt's house used to be. It's nothing but flat land now, covered in sand.

"Yeah, I think all of us needs a break, don't you?"

"You guys should come to Jersey. Clubhouse is being built, no cut-slut drama—"

"Yet," I finish for him.

A RUTHLESS CHRISTMAS

"Doesn't mean I have to be happy about it. I don't miss cut-sluts, man."

"Neither do we. See any of them here? After Candy and Jasmine died, the rest of the sluts skipped town."

"Becks too? I mean, she isn't a slut, but she's usually hanging around."

"She's off pursuing her dream or whatever," I say just as we come face-to-face with Wolf. His nose ring catches the light of the sun, and he holds out a few pieces of glass.

"Someone was here. I know I saw them."

"Fucking hell, does this shit ever stop?" I flip the glass in my hand, noticing the curve of the lens. It's thick and has a bit of weight to it.

"You guys have bad omens," Wolf says, glancing around the clubhouse as if he can see the evil encasing us.

"Not you too! Do not bring that voodoo shit here!" Tool yells from where he's propped up against his bike.

Nothing ever gets better than hearing Tool get freaked out about the supernatural.

"We need to call a meeting," Boomer informs me as he lifts a piece of glass toward the sun.

"We call a meeting for everything these days." I just want to sit on my ass with my pregnant ol' lady with my hand on her belly as we watch B-rated movies on Netflix. People ask me what I want for the holidays? I say, 'nothing.' The truth, though? I want silence.

Quiet.

I want a day where, for once, things aren't complete chaos here at the clubhouse. I don't want danger surrounding us. I don't want another family member showing up out of the blue, and I don't want to find fucking glass littering the property. I don't want Poodle's dog to die of cancer.

One day. All I'm asking is one day for us to fucking *be*.

No threats. No medical emergencies. No panic.

Just happiness. I want us to sit around our Christmas cactus and open gifts. I want bad Christmas music on, and I want to hear all of us laugh at the dumb gifts we get each other.

There's always something going on, and I just want there to be nothing. I want our only worry to be cleaning up wrapping paper.

But that would be too easy.

Just like it would be easy to tell Sarah her tests came back, and it's positive—

she's pregnant—but that isn't the Ruthless way, is it?

How do I tell a woman who has been wanting nothing more than to get pregnant, that her tests are inconclusive? What I do know is I'm telling Reaper and Sarah away from knowing eyes. This has to be done in private.

It's going to be a hopeless Christmas if these pieces of glass have any say in it.

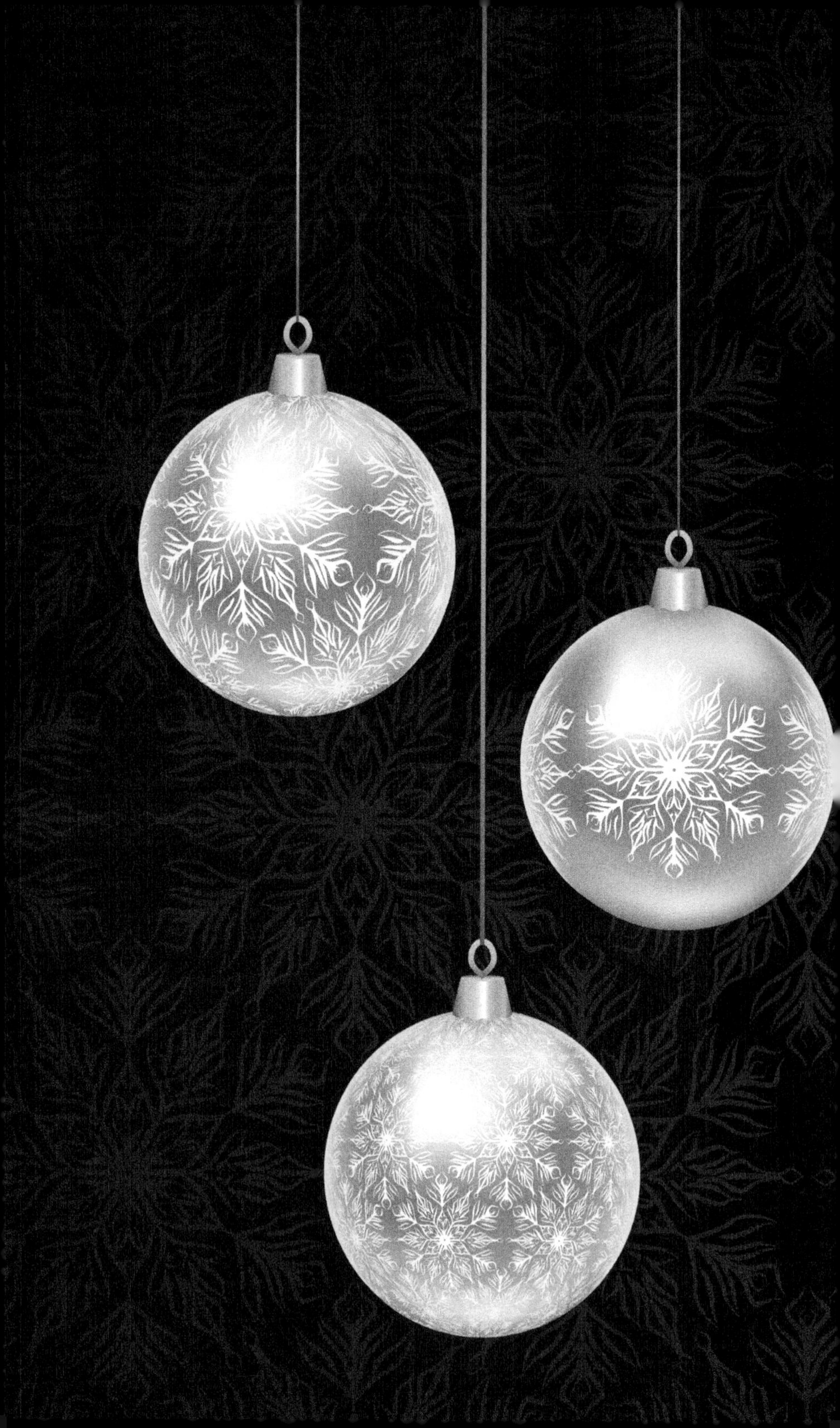

CHAPTER TWELVE

The Groundskeeper

So, what? I almost got caught. No big deal.

I found a new tree. It's more shaded than the last and bonus, it looks like the electric box to the gate is right below me. "Oh, now what do we have here?" I say to myself, leaning forward when I notice movement coming from the front door. I bring my new binoculars to my eyes

"Oh, the days love blessing me with opportunity, don't they?" I see the woman of my dreams leaving the house, Sarah, followed by Patrick.

Hmmm, now that is an interesting combination. Neither of them goes anywhere together unless they're all going somewhere in a big group. She's wearing a beautiful burgundy sweater dress that highlights her blonde hair with black leggings and boots, but the outfit is ruined with that damn 'Property of Reaper' cut. They climb into a new Ford Bronco SUV with Patrick in the front seat.

Tsk. Tsk.

Alcoholics should never be allowed to drive. Even the ones who are 'on a journey' to sobriety. Let's face it. They're never really sober. They're a disaster waiting to happen. He's probably fighting the urge to pour a bottle down his throat. He'd probably eat the glass if given the opportunity.

Pathetic.

And I am not going to let his addiction hurt Sarah.

The bark of the tree bites against my palms as I climb down the trunk. There are a few notches for me to place my feet. When I'm halfway down, I jump, then roll on the ground so I don't make any noise. A few twigs snap, but I could be an animal for all they know.

Who am I kidding? I am an animal.

I slither through the bare bones of trees, ducking under the long fingers of the branches, and bypassing large rocks. I need to figure out a plan. I only wanted Sarah, but Patrick would be fun to torment. This will be one of the only times I will get her alone. She's always with Reaper and surrounded by protection.

Why isn't she now?

I snort and laugh at myself, stretching out my arms, and my hands glide across the body of the tree trunks. Why am I questioning this? This is what I wanted.

Only I'm going to make her see just what kind of people she surrounds herself with and how they aren't good for her. I thought Daphne was better, but I had made a mistake. She's just as rotten as Tongue is on the inside.

Can no one see how horrible these bikers are? What do I need to do to take the blinders off their eyes?

One by one, I'll take them out. It's only a matter of time.

A RUTHLESS CHRISTMAS

I finally get to my car that I pulled into the woods and pull out my bolt cutters. I make my way back to the box just in time to see them pull through the gate. I cut the wire coming from the bottom and the buzz of electricity hums to a slow stop.

I smirk.

Good luck getting to us in time, Kings.

Turning, I run for my car again. I have to get there fast if I'm going to get there before Pirate and Sarah drive by. I'm rounding the front when my foot slips on the sand. I catch myself on the hood of the car, and my forehead smacks against the bumper when my foot keeps slipping. "Son of a bitch!" I groan and hold my hand against the aching spot throbbing in the middle of my forehead.

No, I have to hurry, so I still have time. Time to do, what? I have no idea, but I'll figure it out.

My phone dings, and I see it's a message from Zain.

We're going out for supplies. When you get home, don't be surprised if no one is there. We'll be back soon.

A catlike grin sweeps over my face as I read the message just as another comes through.

You better not be at the Ruthless compound. Reaper is letting me rent this place for a great deal because it needs work. He doesn't know I know you, the guy who nearly killed his members. I won't keep covering for you. Stop with the obsession.

"Stop with the obsession," I mock him as I open the door to the old Lincoln car that someone's grandma used to drive. She's dead. It isn't like she needs it anymore. I punch the dice hanging on the rearview mirror and start the car. They are pink and fuzzy. Cute.

I bet Sarah would like them.

Inserting the silver key in the car, the 1970s radio plays static through the busted speakers, but then the hint of a Christmas song comes sneaking through the white noise.

Oh, the weather outside is certainly very frightful.

And the fire rushing through my veins is, well…

It's delightful

Smirking at the convenient tune, I press my foot on the gas and inch forward. I turn the wheel so I'm facing the long stretch of empty road. I whistle, waiting to see the Ford Bronco pass me. I roll down my window and patiently wait. I stay far enough in the woods where they can't see me, and since I'm less than a half-mile down the road and across the street, they aren't going to expect me.

The grumble of the Bronco engine comes close as I whistle the tune on the radio. There's not much in the desert we can do to make it snow, but the melody brightens my spirits anyway. When the Bronco passes, I put the car in drive and creep out of the woods. The tires dip before getting onto the road, burning some of the rubber when I punch the gas too quick as I crank the wheel.

"Oops," I say when I run over a cactus.

It isn't like we don't have plenty of them in Vegas.

I trail behind the Bronco for a couple of minutes before I decide I'm bored. I want to get the show on the road. I hate being incognito. I've never been good at it. When I want something, I tend to get it.

Even if it means burying my own brother on Halloween, torturing his lover to see what a big mistake she's making, or showing Sarah that she's the sun and the moon, and she deserves the stars. I'll do whatever it takes to take what's mine.

I gas the car, putting the pedal to the metal and cackle when the speedometer reaches the red lines. I quickly catch up with the Bronco and slam the front end of the Lincoln into the back. I laugh uncontrollably, bouncing in my seat when I see Patrick look in the rearview mirror.

They're going to wish that what I have in store for them meant being buried six feet under, but it isn't.

It's going to be more self-destructive, more of a lesson I hope they learn from.

I slam the against the back end again, and the Bronco fishtails as Patrick loses control of the SUV. Tires burn as the Bronco tries to stay on the ground, but the momentum is too much. They flip in the air twice, then the Bronco lands on its side, slamming against a group of trees with a sickening, thrilling crunch.

I come to a stop and get out of the car, casually. "My goodness, I hope everyone is okay," I fawn in a pretend caring, southern accent. "Whatever shall we do?"

"Kill them," the other side of me sneers.

"Not her," the better part of me pleads.

I watch as smoke comes from the engine and the tires spin, still reeling from the speed they were going on the road. The Christmas song still plays in the Lincoln, and I sing it as I strut over to the passenger side.

"The fire is slowly dying, and my dear…" I whistle the rest of the tune and open the door, seeing Sarah passed out with blood trickling down her forehead. "We're still goodbying."

Patrick is out cold too, a piece of glass embedded in his

thigh and blood trickling from some part of his head. I can't tell since I don't care.

I push a piece of Sarah's blonde hair behind her ear, so silky and soft. "It really is the most wonderful time of the year," I say, marveling the beauty in front of me.

She's going to get the best present of them all.

Me.

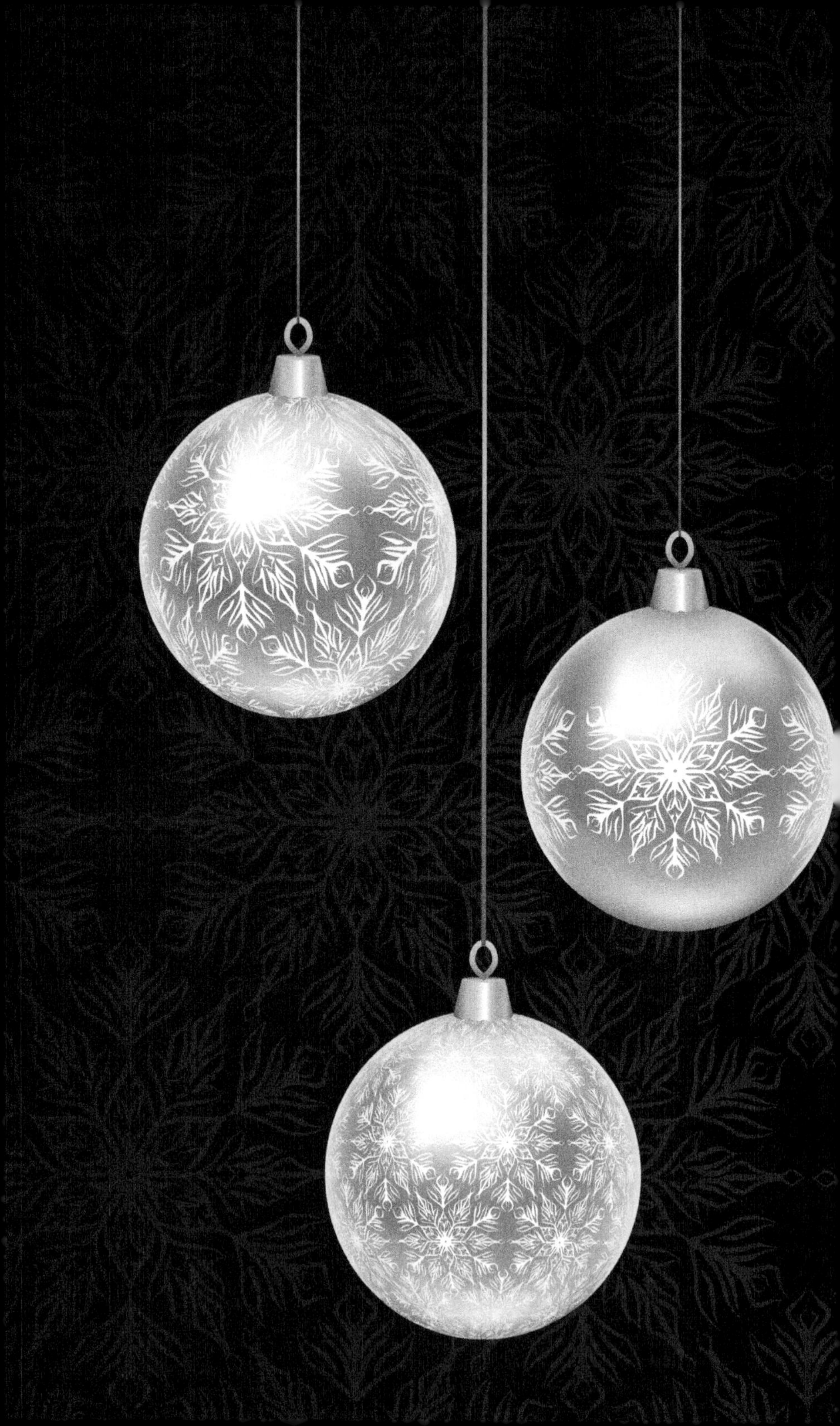

CHAPTER THIRTEEN

Reaper

I KNOW WHEN I HEAR IT.

The sickening sound of metal grinding against metal. The bang and crash of a vehicle rolling. The smell of burning rubber. Time slows when someone hears something like that. It's like the brain can't compute what it heard. It takes a minute to fully understand, to grasp. You have to ask yourself, 'What did I just hear? Is it what I think it is?'

And then comes the sudden silence.

There's no more squealing of tires or shattering glass. There isn't the screech of metal crunching.

Then that's how you know.

And what's worse is when you're running toward the chaos, you don't think there's a chance that someone you love is in the accident.

That's not the case for me.

I know. I know it's Sarah and Patrick. They'd just left, and that loud sound came all too soon. Time is sluggish as I run. I jump down the stairs, Boomer and Tongue at my side, Tool, Knives, Tank, and everyone else following. I pump my arms, trying to move as fast as I can. Fear and panic grip me. My heart can't pump. My lungs are freezing with every ragged breath. My skin is clammy and pale. I trip while I'm running, but Tongue catches me by the back of my cut, saving me from eating dirt. I don't have time to thank him.

My mind is on one thing and one thing only.

Sarah.

We all stop at the gate and grip the iron rods. "Open the fucking gate, Braveheart!" I roar. He presses all sorts of buttons, but it won't open. "Open it!"

"I'm trying, Prez. I swear, I'm trying. It isn't opening," Braveheart explains. He pulls the emergency lever, but even that isn't working. "I don't know why it isn't working! It was fine just a few minutes ago. It opened for them when they left." He runs his hands over his pale face, completely lost on what to do.

I bang my fist against the iron and growl. "Fucking open the goddamn gate, Braveheart!"

"I can't. It won't open, Prez,"

My eyes burn with wild hot flames as I grip the rods in my hands and push with all my might. Everyone catches on, and they stand beside me, grabbing the iron rods and grunting as we dig our feet into the ground.

The gate groans in protest, but inch by inch our feet move as the barrier between me and Sarah finally gives. Sweat drips from my temple, tickling the side of my cheek. I narrow my eyes down the driveway. The dusty road seeming longer than usual, the potholes deeper, the sand thicker.

A RUTHLESS CHRISTMAS

When one of the hinges snaps, the gate swings away. All of us break free, racing down the road. "No, please, no," I whisper a silent prayer to myself and whatever power there is bigger than me. I'm not the religious type, but right now, I'd get on my knees and pray to God.

It's Christmas. This isn't supposed to happen.

When we finally get to the road, all of us come to an abrupt halt. I nearly double over when I look to see the SUV about a half-mile down the road and on its side, smoking. "Sarah!" I yell her name, sprinting down the road. My boots clobber the pavement, and the closer I get to the wreckage, the further away she seems.

"Patrick!" Tongue yells for our brother. I feel like an ass for forgetting that he was with Sarah.

My main concern is her.

The engine is making an awful ticking noise as if it's about to blow.

Fuck.

"Get back!" Boomer screams at us. He turns on his heel and launches in the opposite direction of the car.

I'm the only one who doesn't listen to a man who blows things up for fun. Everyone bolts in the opposite direction. Everyone besides me runs away.

No. I run straight for it.

If Sarah is in that car, I want to die too.

"Come on!" Boomer and someone else grabs me by the shoulders and yanks me back.

"No!" I cry out as they drag me back. I fight against them to throw myself onto the wreckage to be with her.

Through life and death our love will survive.

The boom of fire and force fling us backward. The heat is almost too much to bear as it cloaks my body. The power of the explosion slams us against the ground. I land on my back and hit my head against the pavement. My ears ring, my eyes sting from the fire igniting the SUV, and it's hard to breathe from the smoke lingering in the air. I crawl to my hands and knees and scream.

"No! Sarah! Doll! Sarah!"

I scream for her, my voice hoarse and ragged, hoping she can hear me through the blaring blaze.

"Reaper." Boomer holds me back again from getting closer to the SUV.

I turn, sneering at him to let me go, but he has tears in his eyes too.

"She's gone."

"No! No, she isn't. She isn't gone," I yell, stumbling away from him. How can he give up so easy? Boomer's tears are silent as they fall down his cheek. The orange of the fire flickers in his eyes, a wicked reflection that shows my hell.

"I've never hated fire so much in my entire life," he mutters just before a sob reaches his throat.

This time, it's my heart that's been yanked from my chest. It's my soul that's been reaped.

We were a family. What am I going to tell Maizey? What am I going to do? I can't raise another kid on my own. My chest tightens, and I can't breathe. My left arm tingles, and my heart feels like it's about to explode. I fall to my knees, clutching my chest, where I no doubt believe the organ I harvest from others is being harvested from me.

"Reaper! Hey, Reaper? Call Doc! Call 911, fucking

A RUTHLESS CHRISTMAS

something!" Boomer yells at the guys surrounding us. "Reaper, what's going on? What the fuck is happening!" he screams the last sentence so loud his voice cracks.

Sirens churn the air somewhere in the distance. The scalding torch from the fire feels like it's melting my skin, but I can't seem to care.

Sarah's dead.

And if she's dead, then I don't give a fuck about living. Let me burn, let me turn to ash—let me be nothing but a memory.

But damn it, just let me be with her.

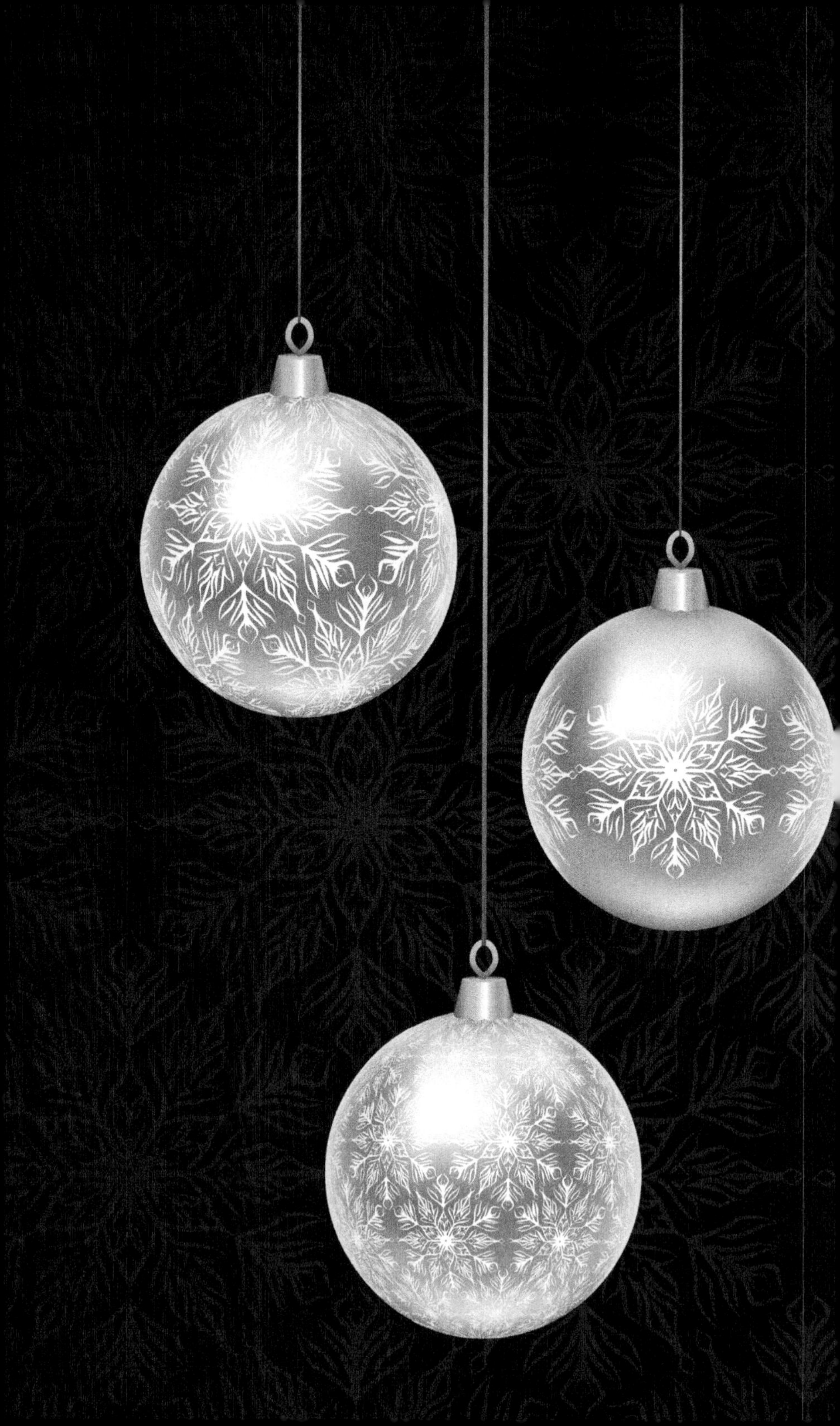

CHAPTER FOURTEEN

Sarah

I'm drowsy. My head is spinning, and no matter how hard I try, I can't open my eyes. I groan when I notice every part of me is in pain. What happened? I manage to pry my lids open, blinking to clear the blur. I can't see anything.

Squeezing my eyes closed, I take a deep breath and try again. I can see clearer this time. I don't know where I am. It isn't the basement or a hospital. It's run down and old. The walls are cracked, the paint is chipping, and the floor is cold, gray, and hard like stone.

Cement.

It's also cracked, with stains. I can only imagine what they are.

A painful moan comes from my left, and that's when I see Patrick. He has a piece of glass in his thigh, blood staining his blue jeans.

The accident.

Someone rear ended us, and Patrick lost control of the vehicle.

"Patrick!" I call out his name and try to run to him, but a thick, clear glass barrier is between us, stopping me. I bang on it with my fists, then squat to get to his level since he's still lying on the floor. "Patrick, get up. Get up. Come on."

He groans again and finally rolls to his uninjured side, leaving the leg straight that has the glass shard in it. "Sarah?"

"I'm here. I'm here, Patrick. Are you okay?"

"I've been better," he jokes, then staggers to his feet. Dragging his leg behind him, he comes to the other side of the wall and presses his hand against it. "Where are we?"

"I don't know. It looks abandoned."

"It's the asylum," Patrick recognizes.

"You're sure?"

"No, but it's the only place I can think of," Patrick says. "It's old, rundown, and the rusty wheelchair in the corner is giving me creepy vibes."

A sad chuckle bubbles in my throat. "I'll have to agree."

"Are you okay? You're bleeding. Prez is going to kill me."

"You're in worse shape than me."

"I've dealt with worse."

The sound of a door opening to the room has us turning. Patrick tries to get as close as he can to the glass to protect me, but he can't. While he takes a step forward to challenge whoever brought us here, I take a step back. The further away from this freak, the better.

He comes into a front area just outside of both of our cells. And he's wearing a baby mask. It's clear, showing the

A RUTHLESS CHRISTMAS

flesh colored tone of his skin, but the design camouflages what he looks like. "Can't even show your face?" I spit. "Coward."

"Oh, so feisty," he says, lacing his hands behind his back as he steps forward. "And so beautiful. Sarah, Sarah, Sarah."

I don't like that he knows my name. And the way he says it sounds like he's finding pleasure in saying it.

"So young and beautiful to be with men like the Kings. I'm here to show you the fault of your ways. To show you that the good in these people you surround yourself with is fake. I'm as real as it gets, Sarah."

His words lodge a weight of fear in my belly, causing the nausea to churn tenfold. "And you think, what? That I'm better off with you? I'd never be with you. I'd rather—"

Our kidnapper slams his hands against the door. "You'd rather what?" His spit sprays against the rectangular window. "You'd rather die than be with someone like me? You're surrounded by people like me. I mean, look at the man next to you. He's a drunk."

"He is not!"

"It's okay, Sarah. He's taunting you," Patrick says, trying to get me to calm down.

"I'm telling her the truth!" The man bangs his fist against the door, and I jump. Bile creeps its way up my throat. I want to throw up. All the horrible smells are getting to me. The dust clinging to the air, the mold along the walls, the rotten stench surrounding us; I can't handle it. "She deserves truth, not constant lies."

"Who are you?" My voice trembles. "What do you want? Money? We have plenty of money."

He tosses his head back and laughs. The column of his throat is thick, and his large Adam's apple bobs. He is in shape. His arms bulge and his chest is wide, which tells me he's strong. "I want you to see the truth," he says. "I don't want money. Money isn't important to me." His hand splays against the window. "But you are. The biker life isn't for a woman like you, Sarah. I've tried so hard to kill a few of them off, to better the world, but no on will fucking die!"

"Oh my god," I stumble backward. "You buried Tongue! You tried to drown Knives! And Daphne…"

"I'm going to fucking kill you!" Patrick slams his body against the metal door, but the metal doesn't even creak or give from the weight of him.

"You'll never be able to get me. You know what these rooms are? These are the insanity rooms. It's what I call them." He starts to pace, slowly, dragging his finger along the walls. "These are the rooms the crazies go in, the ones who constantly scream, the ones who cry, who hurt themselves. The ones who have to get strapped down. The ones who wear the straitjacket." He turns around and walks toward me.

Patrick watches him like a hawk, following The Groundskeeper's every step.

"So many evil things happened in these rooms," he continues, lowering is voice. The octave sends shivers down my spine. "I read one man banged his head against the glass so many times, he killed himself." He tsks, as if he cares. "Shame."

But he doesn't.

"If you look, you'll see the crack. Right there." He points in my cell, and I follow where he's pointing his finger.

A RUTHLESS CHRISTMAS

When I see the point of impact, I lose any control I had over my stomach and vomit.

"Sarah, are you okay?"

"I'm fine," I say to Patrick.

"The baby?" Patrick asks, and I know it's to see if I feel any pain. I don't. Yet.

"Baby? You're pregnant?" The Groundskeeper bangs his fist against the door. "I'll get it out of you. Don't worry. You won't ever have to deliver a biker's baby."

I scoot back until I hit the wall, holding my stomach protectively. If I am pregnant, there is no way in hell I'm going to let this man touch me. What scares me even more is how sincere he looks as he stares at me, like he genuinely cares and believes in this mission that he's on.

"First things first," he says, lifting up a bottle of whiskey.

"No!" I shake my head, realizing what he's about to do. I turn to look at Patrick, who's watching The Groundskeeper unscrew the cap to the bottle, fingers clenched in his palm and chest heaving. He's already fighting himself. "Don't do this. I'll go with you. Okay? I'll go, just leave Patrick alone."

"Don't you mean, Pirate? I'm sure after all of this, he's thirsty." The Groundskeeper walks in front of Patrick's door and pours some whiskey on the floor. "You can't be a pirate without a nice swig of whiskey. Isn't that right, Pirate?"

Patrick's reaction is immediate. His nostrils flare, and he falls forward, catching himself on his fists as he tries to control the disease swirling inside him.

"Patrick, don't give in. You can do this. Think about Sunnie. Think about her. Hold onto that."

"This smells so good," The Groundskeeper says, almost

with a sexual gratification. His eyes close as he inhales, and Patrick's eyes stare at the bottle with want and need. "Watch him fall apart, Sarah. Watch him and let him so you know just how weak the Kings really are." He places the bottle in the middle of the room and walks out the door, locking it behind him.

The buzzer sounds, and automatically Patrick's door swings open to allow him in the main room where the bottle waits for him.

"Sarah…" whispers Patrick, a desperate hinge to his voice that's begging me to save him.

Patrick finds the furthest corner in his cell and sits. His shirt is drench in sweat, and he licks his lips as if he can taste the alcohol. He buries his hand in his jean pocket and pulls out his sobriety chip, bringing it to his mouth and holding it against his lips. I hope he can taste the victory on the small token because it's the only thing keeping him grounded.

I thought the biggest villain was The Groundskeeper, but he isn't.

It's the square bottle with a narrow neck sitting on the floor, the burning smell of whiskey hanging in the air, and the temptation to get drunk. Patrick's damnation is only a few feet away, and the only thing stopping him from giving in is control.

And it's fragile enough that it can break at any moment.

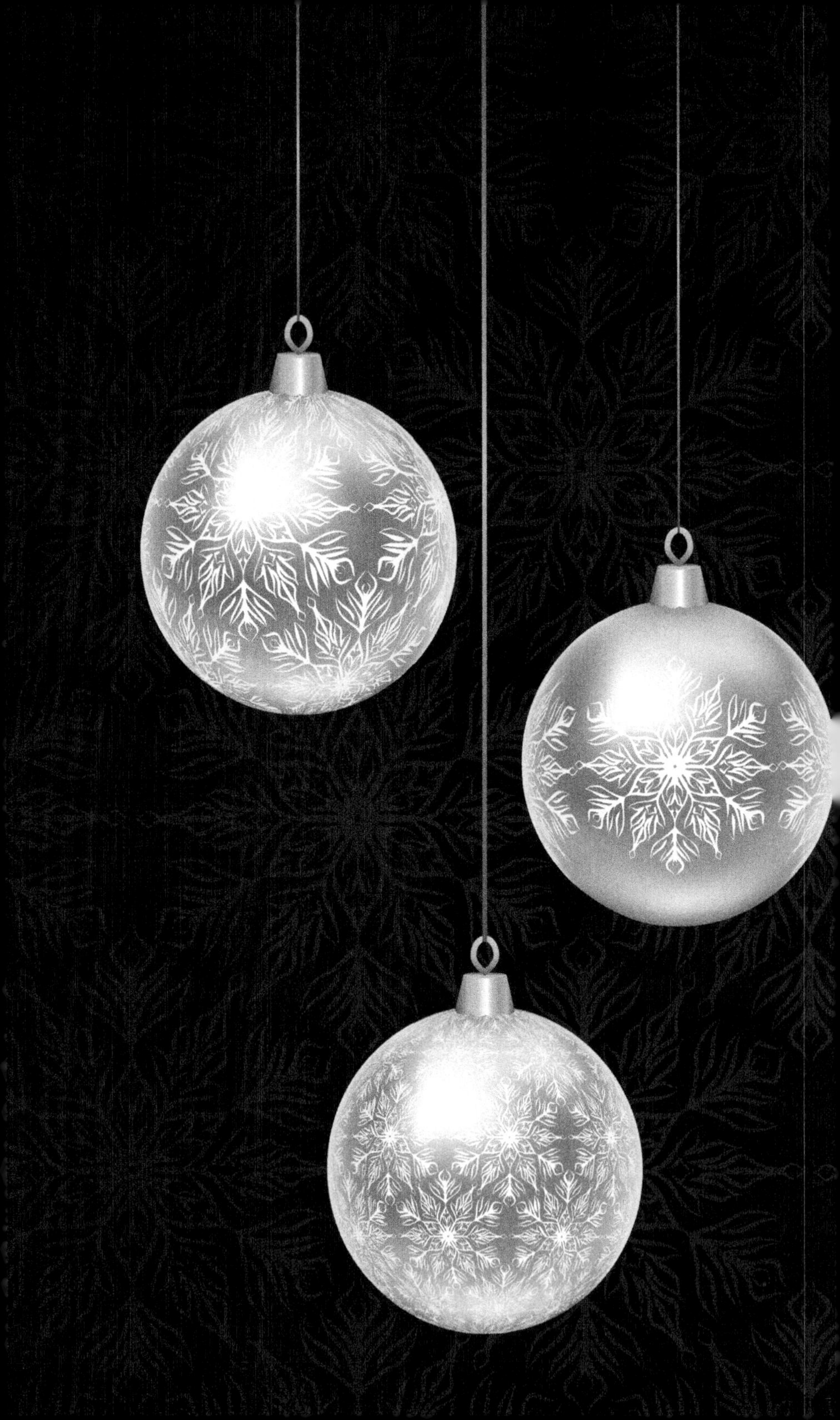

CHAPTER FIFTEEN

Zain

WHAT DID PORTER DO?

I know he needs help. I do. He has an identity issue that he has yet to be able to come to terms with. He isn't all there upstairs, but I guess that's the story for all of us here at the asylum. We're all fucked up in the head. Some are worse than others, like me. My mania controls who I am half the time. The battle inside me is loud, a constant bomb ready to blow, until I'm left gasping for air.

Peeking around the corner of the wall, I see him watching through the window of the door that used to allow doctors and nurses to check in on their patients without having to interact. This part of the house, this wing, it's closed off for a reason. It's too far away from the main branch of the house because this is where the doctors ran all of their illegal experiments.

Why did I choose to live here?

Because this house is unwanted just like the rest of us. When Porter reached out to me about this place, all of us were homeless, and we banded together to make sure we were protected. Then I found out where it was and who owned it, and I thought there would be no hope.

Jesse is my nephew, the President of the Ruthless Kings. He never got to meet me, and I never got to meet him. My brother had nothing to do with me because of my mental state. I was too much to deal with, too much of a hassle for my family. I've always been on my own, and when I explained all of that to Reaper, he graciously had me sign a contract, handed me the keys to the house, and invited me over for Christmas.

I could have a family, one with blood. I want that. I crave that. I'm a lunatic, a havoc, a broken soul, and I've found the birds of my flock. That doesn't mean I don't yearn for more.

If I'm not honest with Reaper, if I let Porter keep doing this, we'll end up homeless again. Or we'll be dead. I have a feeling Reaper isn't the forgiving type.

"It's just a matter of time," Porter says to himself before walking away. His footsteps echo down the hall. When he's far enough away to where I can't hear them anymore, I peek inside to see what he was looking at, and my mania roars its ugly head.

I swing my head back and forth, gripping the trim of the door. He kidnapped Sarah. I don't know the other guy, but this isn't right. This isn't right!

I can't open it because I don't know if I can trust myself once I'm in there. I might destroy anything and everything in my path.

A RUTHLESS CHRISTMAS

Including Sarah.

I push off the wall and know exactly what I have to do. Like a pissed off bull, I charge down the hallway until I'm at the front of the house where the others are. They're sitting on the floor since we don't have furniture.

"Where are you going, Zain?" Apollo asks. I don't know if that's his real name, but I know he's delusional. He believes he is Apollo, a divinity, a God. He doesn't believe he is God, but a Greek God.

And honestly, I'm not sure which one is more dangerous.

"Porter."

"Again?" He stands, wiping off his jeans. "Want me to come with you?"

"No. There are two people he kidnapped in the forbidden wing. Two people who belong to the Kings. I'm telling Reaper. I don't care what you have to do—you put Porter in a room he cannot get out of; do you hear me?" I don't say another word. I know Apollo won't let me down.

I dig for the car keys in my pocket and notice how damaged the Lincoln is. "Damn it, Porter. Damn it!" I punch the hood of the car with both hands, denting it further, and try to take deep breaths like my therapist said. As long as I can control the outrage, I might not experience a full-blown episode, which I can hardly remember when it happens.

Porter is trying to ruin everything we want for ourselves, but I'm not going to let him. I climb into the Lincoln Continental, and the engine clicks as if it's about to die, but I pull out of the driveway and take the road leading to the compound. All I can hope is I don't get killed by my nephew.

The miles of desert on either side get my heart racing. I don't like to be in big spaces; they make me feel lost and alone. I swallow, keeping my eyes forward on the road. I tighten my fingers around the wheel until the leather squeaks.

A Christmas song tries to play through the busted speakers, but all it does is grate my nerves, so I turn down the volume until all I hear is the scrap of the bumper on the road and the hum of the tires.

Ten minutes later I get to the Ruthless Kings clubhouse, but an ambulance is there, along with firetrucks and cop cars. I park on the side of the road and open the driver's side door. Immediately, I'm hit with the smell of smoke, and I see Reaper shoving the paramedics off him. It's chaos, something Porter loves to create.

"What did you do?" I ask, knowing Porter can't answer me. I can't protect him from this. I'm not sure what his obsession with the Kings is, but it has to come to an end.

"Get off me! I'm fucking fine."

"Sir, you had a mild heart attack. We need to get you to the hospital," the paramedic yells and when I hear that, I run toward the wreck. Water splashes under my feet from the firefighters putting out the flames coming from the car. The smoke makes me cough, but the sorrow on my nephew's face makes me want to kill Porter.

As much as I want to kill him, I've seen Porter on medication, and he can be a good man. He needs help. I won't give up on him, even if he does deserve it.

"I don't give a fuck. Get off me!" Reaper shoves the medic again and staggers to his feet.

A RUTHLESS CHRISTMAS

"The car is empty," the firefighter informs everyone at once.

Reaper turns around, hope on his face as he stares at the firefighter. "It's empty. You're sure?"

"Positive. There are no crispy skeletons in there," the guy says casually as he walks to the firetruck.

"Guys, they might be alive." Reaper grins, tears shining in his eyes. "Alive."

This is my chance. I step forward, cutting through the men in leather until Reaper can see me. "They're alive, and I know where they are."

In a second, Reaper has his hand wrapped around my throat. I expect the cops to do something, to aim their guns and to order Reaper to stop choking me, but no one does anything. Reaper has Vegas in his pocket for good reason.

I don't want to be the outsider.

"Tell me," he sneers. "Uncle or not, I'll fucking kill you."

I gasp, my face heating from the trapped blood. "They're at the asylum. It's Porter. He did it."

Reaper lets go, and I gasp, clawing at my throat and coughing to try to breathe. He holds a hand against his heart, and the medics come to his side again, but he pushes them away. "Get the fucking point. I am refusing medical treatment."

"Your funeral, dude," a small man with a feminine voice says to Reaper as he shuts the doors to the back of the ambulance.

"You need us, Reaper?" a cop asks, just as another member, Badge, hands him a stack of cash.

"No, this is club business," Reaper growls, his eyes like slits as he stares at me.

If I don't make this right, I'm a dead man.

"Okay. Call if you need us." The cop whistles and rounds up his officers. They climb in their patrol cars, turn off their sirens, and drive away. Badge hands over a stack of cash to the firefighters too and then to the medics.

"Are you buying my silence?" The gay medic sounds insulted; at least, I'm assuming he's gay.

"You can pay with your life if you want?" Badge suggests, slapping the cash against the guy's chest.

"It's been a pleasure doing business with you."

"It means you're who we call. You work for us now," Badge says.

"Honey, I work for the hospital. Until my paycheck says big bad bikers on it in the left-hand corner, I do not work for you." The guy struts toward the driver's side door, hops in, and waves goodbye as he drives off.

Little man has big balls. Good for him. I think.

You can kill him. Release it and you can kill all of them.

I scratch my fingers against the bumpy road, letting the skin peel and blood drip. Inflicting pain reminds me that I'm just as human as anyone else. I can control me. I am the control.

"Who the fuck is Porter?" Reaper snarls, his boots blocking my line of sight as I lay on the ground.

"You know him as The Groundskeeper. He has an identity disorder—" I don't get to finish my explanation because my tongue is being pulled from my mouth, and a knife is threatening to cut it off.

A RUTHLESS CHRISTMAS

"Tongue, don't. He has answers, and he won't be able to give us information if he has no tongue."

The metallic taste of blood bursts across my taste buds. I can tell the man isn't happy with his Prez's order, but I'm appreciative because it causes him to pull away. "That man buried me, nearly killed Knives, kidnapped Daphne, and now Patrick and Sarah? We've killed for less."

"You knew? About Porter, you know him?"

I swallow, the cut on my tongue stinging with pain. "I've known him since we broke out of the mental institution we were in. He's a good guy on the right meds. We're all fucked up, Reaper."

"I want retribution," Reaper growls. "No one takes Sarah and lives to tell the tale."

"He's sick, Reaper. He's sick."

"Once I rip his heart out, he won't have to worry about it anymore. Take me to the asylum. Now."

"Reaper, I need to make sure your heart is okay," a blond guy with looks that tells me he isn't meant to be here warns Reaper.

"Later Doc. If Sarah isn't okay, then you'll have your answer."

Porter better hope he hasn't harmed a hair on their heads. The only way I can save Porter is if Sarah and Patrick are okay.

"Reaper, I don't know if she's pregnant. The test came back inconclusive."

The blood drains from my face when I hear that bit of news. Sarah could be pregnant.

"Let's hope she isn't, or this stress will cause another

miscarriage," Reaper mutters. A few trucks pull out of the compound's driveway, coming to pick us up to go to the asylum. Tongue grips me by my shirt and lifts me to my feet.

Another?

Porter, what did you do?

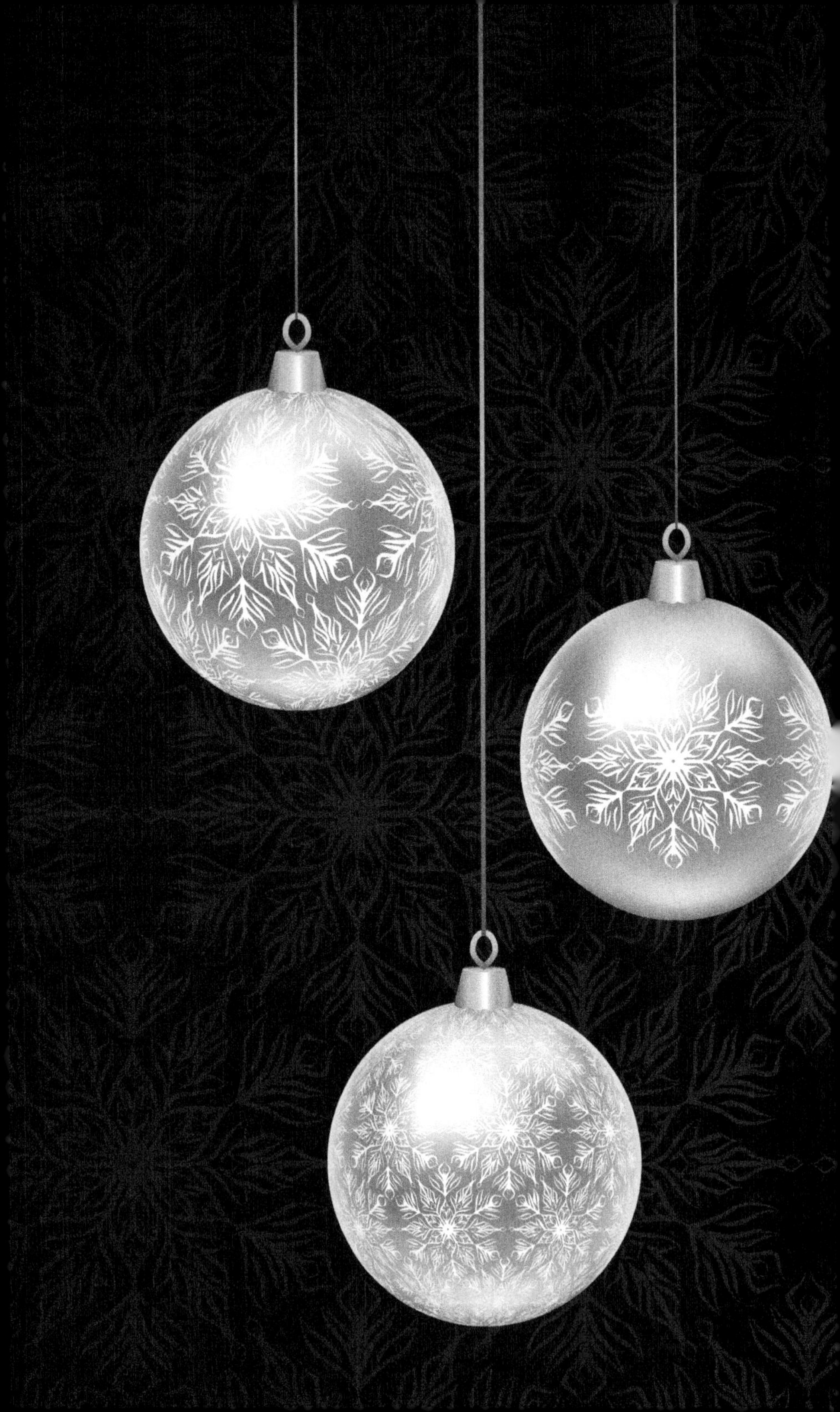

CHAPTER SIXTEEN

Patrick

THE WHISKEY SMELLS SO GOOD. I CAN ALMOST FEEL IT SLIDING down my throat. I can almost feel the burn, feel it pool like a puddle of gasoline in my stomach. I'm shaking, trembling, and my mouth won't stop watering. I really thought I was stronger than this, but I haven't been tested since I got out of rehab. Everyone has been so supportive by keeping the alcohol away from me that my will hasn't been tried.

Well, it is now.

And it feels like my skin is burning, crawling with need. There's a voice inside my head, encouraging me to take one sip. Only one. The last one ever. The chance to say goodbye. I can do that. There's no harm in one more taste. If I think about it, I never really got to have one last drink because I didn't know it would be 'the last' one.

"Patrick, talk to me. Tell me what you're feeling. Don't give in," Sarah says, placing her hand against the glass.

I bury my head between my knees and my fingers along the cold cement I'm sitting on. I need Sunnie. I need her so bad right now. "I forgot how good it smells," I admit, unable to look Sarah in the eye after saying the words. "I wish Sunnie was here." I tilt my head back until I hit the wall, closing my eyes so I don't have a constant view of the bottle sitting in the middle of the room outside my door.

Grabbing the bottom of my shirt, I lift it and wipe the sweat off my face. I almost feel like I'm in rehab again, only this time I'm not detoxing; I'm holding myself back from relapsing.

"Think about her. Think about how worried she is about you, Patrick. Think about rehab and everything you've been through, okay? You're stronger than the temptation. You're stronger than the whiskey."

I try to listen to Sarah and take a few deep breaths in, but that backfires because I can nearly taste the whiskey in the air. I hit my knuckles against the ground, over and over until I feel the skin split. With every slam, the pain becomes worse.

The pain might be the only thing stopping me from giving in and chugging the entire bottle.

So much for having a nice Christmas with everyone. I should have known. It's always something.

Right about now, when I'm craving a shot and the high only alcohol can give me, Sunnie reads that ridiculous romance novel to me. Samuel and Elizabeth. I almost know the damn thing by heart, word for word, but it's my safety net. A symbol of faith, love, and hope. Sunnie read that to me when I was at my lowest. When I hated everything in the world, even her.

A RUTHLESS CHRISTMAS

She never gave up on me. She read that damn novel to me, and honestly, it wasn't the story that calmed me but the sound of Sunnie's voice. It was the way she read, her tone, and how effortless she spoke. She's my sun on a fucking stormy day, and I need her now more than ever.

The need to drink is clawing at my gut.

"What would Sunnie do?" Sarah asks.

For some reason it makes me laugh because I think of the 'What would Jesus do?' slogan.

WWSD.

I need that tattooed on my damn body.

"She'd read to me," I say.

"I don't have a book."

"It's okay. There's only one that will work anyway, and Sunnie has it. She takes it everywhere. I know the first few chapters by heart."

"Stop hitting the ground and tell me the story, Patrick."

I open my eyes and stare at her like she's crazy, but she has fear written all over her face. Her mouth is pinched, her brows are furrowed, and she plasters herself against the glass to try to get as close as possible to me.

"Tell me the story," she says again.

My cheeks flame with embarrassment. It's my secret with Sunnie. I suppose secrets don't matter anymore. Not when it comes to health. I tighten the sobriety chip in my palm and nod. I can do this. I can win.

"Elizabeth hated wearing a corset under her dress. The last thing she believed women should do was hurt themselves for beauty. Making a smaller waistline was not for her; it was for them—for men. Her lungs protested all day. Her breasts were pushed so high she was surprised they didn't touch her chin, but she had to deal with the fashions of a lady. Even if she didn't consider herself one."

Sarah giggles. "I'm sorry; I don't mean to laugh. It never thought you were the type to read regency romance."

"I don't read it. Only one story is read to me. It's different." Plus, it helps curve the urge, and isn't that all that matters? Thinking about reciting the next few sentences already has me calming down, the thirst dissipating. I think about rehab and laying in bed, hallucinating that I saw my sister Macy. I screamed, I begged, I cried. I constantly asked for a drink, and all Sunnie did was hold my hand and read me the silly novel she stole from Patricia, an evil bitch I later killed.

I stand on my feet, staggering because of the piece of glass in my thigh. I yank it out. "Fuck, that hurts."

"Where are you going? Stop, Patrick." Sarah bangs her hands against the wall to stop me, but I have a goal. "Patrick, tell me more of the story. Skip to your favorite part!"

I limp through the whiskey spilled on the floor, staring at the bottle standing all alone in the middle of the room. Light shines through the hole in the roof. The glass and liquid amber glimmers beautifully, casting a kaleidoscope of colors along the floor.

If no one thought whiskey in a bottle could be pretty, they were wrong.

"Patrick, please, tell me your favorite part. Do not pick up that whiskey." Sarah is at her door now, staring at me with glassy eyes.

I think about the book, and there was always one part I really liked more than the others. "Samuel is lost in her love and in Elizabeth's fierce independence. She takes on the world with strength he had never seen before with any other woman. She's a rebel, the kind of woman others would deem 'unworthy' of marriage, but Samuel couldn't disagree more. Elizabeth hasn't found a man who is strong enough to match her strength. Until now." I bend over and pick up the open bottle, watching the liquid swish on the inside like an angry sea.

I need to match Sunnie's strength, the kind she's placed in me. She counts on me. I bring the bottle to my nose and inhale. Clutching onto the chip, thinking about Samuel and Elizabeth, and Sunnie's love, I launch the bottle across the room. The glass hits the wall, shattering with the impact, and the whiskey is a tsunami after being released. The wave tries to get to me, but I'm too far away.

I'm safe.

The door kicks in right as I collapse. A pair of arms wrap around me to hold me up. "I got you, Patrick. Sunnie is waiting for you at home," comes Doc's voice. I am still a little lightheaded. But I did it. I didn't drink the whiskey. "Did you—"

"No," I say with a smile. "No."

"So fucking proud of you," Doc informs me and carries me out of the alcohol-infused space. "Sunnie will be too."

"I think I need a meeting, Doc."

"You don't say?" He tilts his lips in a smile as he leans me against the broken desk that's been here since the place was built.

I lean all of my weight on my other leg and watch as Reaper carries Sarah out of the room. When he feels like he has her in a safe space, he falls to his knees and cups the back of her head. He buries his face in her neck, and I know he's either crying or fighting the tears.

"I thought you died. I thought you were fucking dead," he says, wrapping his arms around her so tight, I worry he may to cut off her air supply. "I love you. You can't do that to me. You can't… You just can't." Reaper slams his lips against hers, and all the guys look at me to give Reaper and Sarah their moment.

"I'm glad you're okay," Boomer says.

"Thanks, Boomer. Glad to see you." All of his members are here too, which means he has come for Christmas.

Hell of a ride that's been. I can't wait for the holiday to be over.

"You can't keep me here!" I hear from down the hallway, followed by loud bangs.

"It's the only way your life can be spared, Porter. You have to stay in here until you're better." I limp down the hallway, but an arm helps support my weight.

It's Tongue.

We stand next to Zain, and another bang sounds as Porter keeps smashing his shoulder against the glass. He sees Tongue and becomes angrier. "You! I fucking hate you. I'm going to kill you; you hear me? I'm going to kill you. My dad might have fucked your mom, but we are far from family."

Holy shit.

Tongue's brother is this psychopath?

Christmas gifts keeping flying at us, don't they?

Tongue doesn't seem too surprised. "What are you doing?" Zain asks as Tongue enters the room his brother is in.

A RUTHLESS CHRISTMAS

Now that I see them side by side, there are a few similarities physically, but mentally, both of them are fucked up.

"You know what?" Tongue's voice is slow with gravel and a Southern accent. "I don't give a fuck if you're my blood because all my life you've been nothing to me." Tongue punches Porter across the face, then pulls out his brother's tongue. "You hurt my Comet." Porter tries to get away, but Tongue holds on tighter and grabs his homemade knife.

He places it against the pink appendage and right as he's about to cut, Reaper stops him. "Tongue, don't! He's your family."

"He's no family of mine."

"That's an order."

Tongue slides the knife across the wet muscle until he gets to the middle. "I've never really cared for orders," Tongue snarls and stabs through the middle of his brother's tongue. Blood spills, and Porter screams. He'll still be able to talk, but it will be awhile. Tongue listened to Prez, technically.

He bends over and wipes his knife clean on Porter's pants. Porter spits blood, yelling in agony, but Tongue isn't fazed. "Merry Christmas. Don't say I never gave you anything." Tongue slams the door as he exits the room, then slides the lock bar in place.

"Let's go home," Reaper announces to all of us.

"Yeah, I need to check on your heart."

"Your heart?!" Sarah screeches. "Why? What happened?"

"I thought you died. My heart couldn't handle it. I had a heart attack."

That's the thing about falling in love while you're a Ruthless King. When we fall, we fall fucking hard. And if we ever lose the one thing that gives our dark, fucked up lives meaning, we fall too.

"Promise you'll let Doc check you out?" Sarah begs, worry etched on her young face.

"I'm not coughing."

"That isn't how I check your heart, Reaper."

Tongue and Boomer help me walk out of this hellhole asylum, a psychotic estate I hope to never find myself in again, and everyone laughs at Doc and Reaper's banter. It lightens the mood.

There's still a grey cloud hanging over us, and Christmas won't be what it needs to be until it's gone.

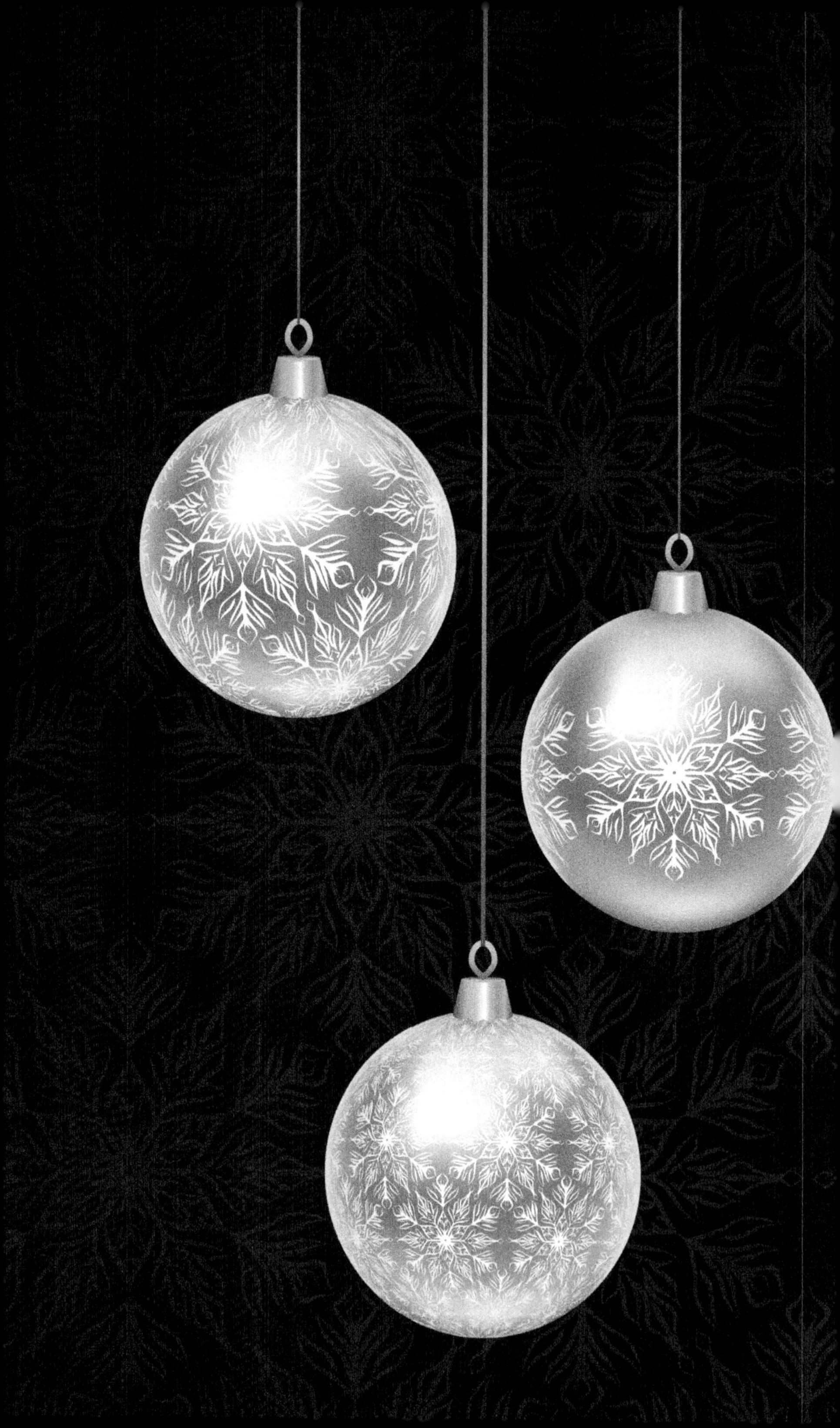

CHAPTER SEVENTEEN

Badge

Christmas Eve

"**N**o glitter, Maizey. You know the rules."

"Badge! Come on; it's Christmas. Glitter will make you look like a snowflake."

I cross my arms over my chest and glare at her. "I don't want to look like a snowflake."

"Putting glitter on you is on my Christmas wish list. See!" She shoves the paper so far in my face that I can't even read it.

Kids are so annoying, but Maizey is okay. I can deal with her. I never want kids of my own, though. Hell no. "I don't want glitter. That's just a wish you're never going to be able to get."

"I'm telling Reaper," Maizey huffs.

"Telling Reaper, what?" Slingshot asks, shoving a taco in his mouth as he stands in the doorway.

"Did you take your pill?" Maizey and I ask in unison as we watch him unwrap another taco from his bag.

"Yes, I took my pill. God, get off my back."

"Ew, Uncle Slingshot. Your back is stinky, 'member?" Maizey curls her nose in disgust, and I can't stop laughing at how serious she looks.

"It is not. You two are mean. I was going to let you put glitter on my face, but forget it. Be that way," Slingshot sharply spins on his heel and walks away, head held high.

Maizey lets out this scream that has my toes curling as my ear drums rumble. She throws her makeup brush down and runs after Slingshot in her princess gown. "Come back, come back, Uncle Slingshot. I didn't mean it."

"You did!" Slingshot argues with a seven-year-old girl.

I shake my head and grab the pink bedazzled mirror to see what Maizey has done to me this time. "Oh God," I groan when I see bright blue eye shadow, pink lipstick, and my hair in small piggy-tails on top of my head.

"You look so pretty," Sarah compliments me, chuckling when she sees my appearance.

She has a bandage on the side of her head still from the accident, but other than that, she looks great. "Do not," I grumble and stand, stretching my arms over my head.

"You're good with her, you know. I know you say you don't like kids but, Badge, you're a natural at it."

"Where's Reaper?" I ask her, wanting to change the subject. I don't like talking about kids. It makes me feel awful, like something is wrong with me when I say I don't want to have a baby. It's just how I feel. Maizey is cute and fun, but at the end of the day, I can give her back when I'm sick of her.

A RUTHLESS CHRISTMAS

Not that I'm ever sick of her, but if I ever was, I could give her back.

Sarah's blonde hair falls in her face as she straightens her body from being perched against the wall. "He went to go pick up the rest of the gifts since Patrick and I were interrupted."

"How are you doing?" I ask softly, and her face falls. She lays her hand on her stomach and takes a minute to compose herself, but the emotion is written all over her face.

Doc told them about the inconclusive test, and Sarah cried for hours. We didn't see her the rest of the night when we brought her home from the asylum.

"I'm okay."

"I know." I bring her in for a hug, and Boomer comes over behind her. He's wearing a Santa hat and has a grenade in his hand. "Boomer?" I draw out his name, wondering what plan he has conjured up.

"Who wants to go blow holes in the sand?"

"Oh, oh, I do! Let me get my shoes on." Sarah claps her hands in excitement. I often wonder how the hell they're related, but then I see shit like this, and it all clicks. "I'm so glad you're here. I love you," she says, giving him a quick hug before she runs to get her shoes.

"Damn, Badge. You look hot."

"Fuck you, Boomer."

"Want to go out sometime? Can I get to second base?"

I push him out of the way, and he slams against the wall, laughing his ass off.

I walk into the living room, catcalls ringing through the air, and I find myself under a mistletoe. Before I can make my escape, a small hand tugs on mine.

It's Maizey.

"What?"

"Pick me up," she orders.

I pick her up by her arms and saddle her to my hip. "No glitter," I warn.

"No glitter," she agrees and gives me a quick peck on the cheek. "Mistletoe kisses instead." Maizey gives me another kiss, and my heart warms from her thoughtfulness.

I place a kiss on her forehead, then set her down on the floor before she's off running again. Everyone's eyes are on me, and I curl my lip, annoyed they saw me vulnerable. "What the hell are you guys looking at?"

"Nothing."

"Not a thing."

"Nice rack," Skirt says, giving me a wink.

I flick Skirt off, and he covers his daughter's eyes with his hand, so she doesn't see. She's five minutes old or something like that. She can't fucking see anyway.

I have to wear the makeup until I go to bed. That's the deal every time. I always have to hear jokes from everyone else. I make my way to the couch and sit next to Poodle, who's petting Lady as she sleeps.

"I'm sorry about Lady." I've must have said that fifty times since he told us about the cancer. Poodle doesn't even look up to see how ridiculous I am with makeup on; he stares at Lady, trying to make her feel better by loving on her with gentle strokes across her belly.

It's going to be a sad day when Lady dies.

I hope Christmas day is filled with joy. It's a day the club really needs. With Lady on her last few days, Sarah maybe

A RUTHLESS CHRISTMAS

not being pregnant, Reaper finding out he has an uncle he doesn't know and a sister he didn't know existed, and Tongue being related to a psycho—which is not surprising—tomorrow needs to be a good day.

It *has* to be.

It's why I've fucking volunteered to be Santa for some damn reason.

What the hell is wrong with me? Why do I do this to myself?

Right. At least I get cookies and milk. That will be worth it.

Because I don't even like kids. I can't stand them.

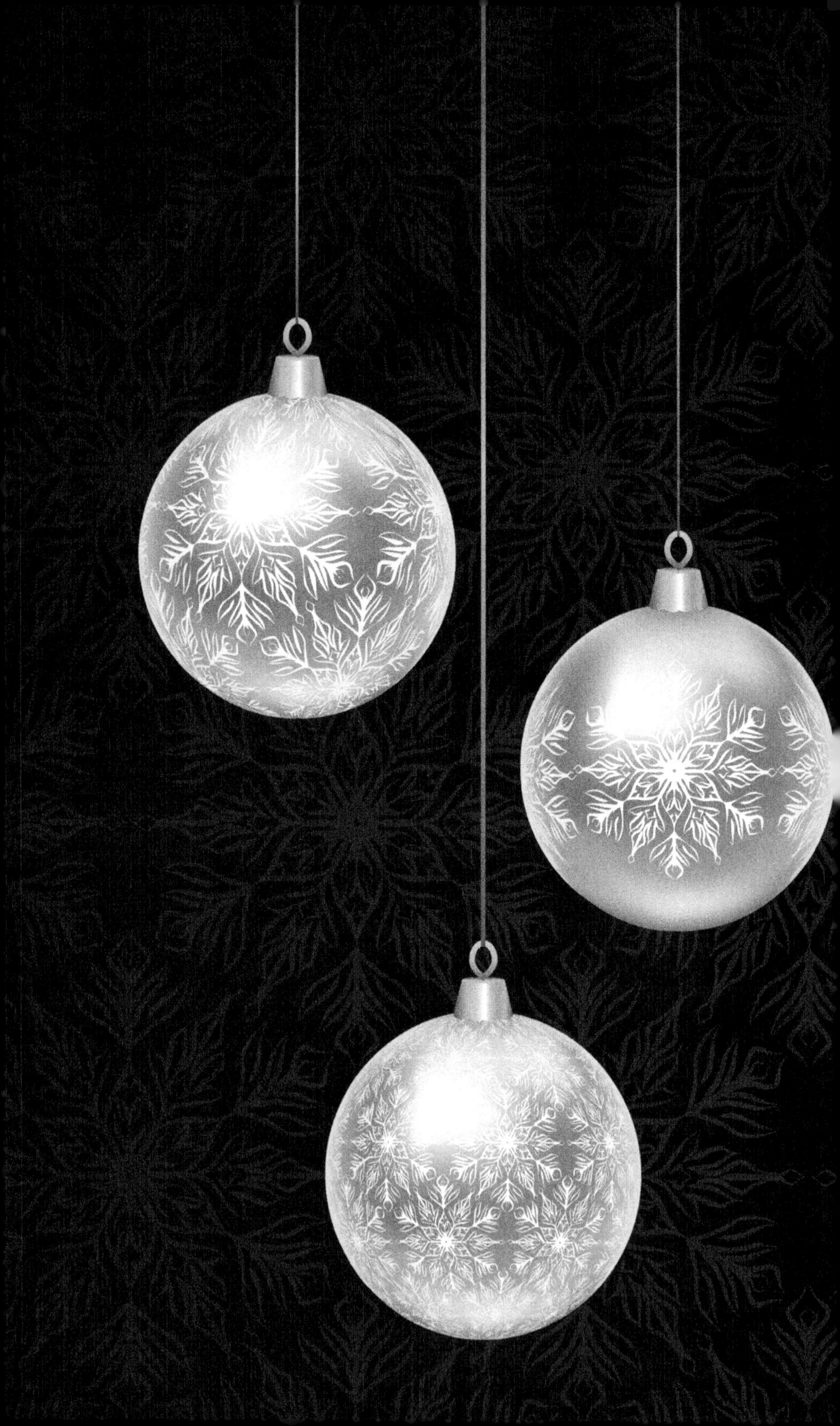

CHAPTER EIGHTEEN

Reaper

It's two in the morning, and Badge looks ridiculous. All the adults are awake, drinking, laughing, and blowing off steam. Sarah is trying to stuff one last pillow in the Santa outfit for Badge's fake belly, but it won't go in.

Oh, wait, never mind. She got it.

She grunts as she pulls the black belt tight and slaps his round belly when she's done. The outfit is complete. "There. You're all done."

"How do I look?" Badge asks everyone in the kitchen. Even my sister is here instead of downstairs. She has stayed next to me all day and night, and that makes me feel good; like she can trust me.

The last few days have been horrible. I never want to experience the horrors I went through thinking Sarah was dead. Doc ran some tests on my heart and come to find out, I didn't have a heart attack, but I did experience broken heart syndrome.

I didn't know that was a thing until Doc told me. My heart was literally broken; the tendons inside were under so much stress from the grief I felt that they snapped.

"You look like a fake Santa," Tongue says, placing Happy on the table.

Everyone scoots back, chairs fall to the floor, and Happy swishes his tail, which has a bell on it, so it jingles every time he moves. Let's not forget the Santa hat and the matching red nails. Daphne isn't scared like the rest of the guys. She's sitting on Tongue's lap and kisses Happy on the snout.

There really is someone out there for everyone.

"Tongue, you do know all Santas are fake," Badge points out, and Tongue whips out his knife and flings it through the air. It takes off Badge's Santa hat and pins it to the wall.

"I'll take that as a 'yes,'" Badge tugs the knife from the wall and readjusts his hat. "Okay, give me the bag. I can't believe I'm doing this," he grumbles as I hand him the heaviest bag of fucking gifts in the world. He grips the red bag and throws it over his shoulder, and Sarah sneaks a picture.

"Sorry, I had to," Sarah says. "Okay, remember, Maizey is going to wake up. She wants proof you're real. Be ready."

"Aidan too. They will work together as a team."

"I'm not scared of kids," Badge stays, shoving a cookie in his mouth. "Kids are dumb. In a good way, you know, innocent and 'growing' and all that." He finger quotes it, which only makes us think he's truly terrified of what's about to happen. Kids are smart, resilient, and clever.

And he has no idea what he's signed up for. "Okay, everyone, quiet down. Not one noise. Badge is going to put the gifts under the tree," I say, flipping the light off, so we're all in the dark. The kitchen is warm with so many bodies in it. On top of the Kings, Boomer and his crew are here too.

Patrick ad Sunnie aren't here. They're in their room. After the emotional ordeal with Patrick fighting off his urge to drink, he's been asleep since. Sunnie hasn't left his side and has read that damn book front to back three times for him, but Sarah told me that's what stopped Patrick from taking a drink. I'll be forever in her debt for saving my friend.

I peek around the corner to see Badge drop the bag on the floor and lay his hands on his stomach. He ho-ho-ho's like Santa does, and I have to cover my mouth to keep quiet. Badge is such an asshole; he loves this shit, no matter how much he says he hates it.

He finds the cookies and milk on the mantel and ignores the gifts for a few minutes. He stuffs the chocolate chip cookies in his mouth, then chugs the milk. When he's done, he grabs the plate of carrots for the reindeer, turns over his shoulder, and points to it. "What the fuck do I do with this?"

"Eat it," I whisper loudly.

"I hate carrots," Badge grumbles his dissatisfaction and tosses the carrots in the fireplace instead. "There. Problem solved."

I rub my hand down my face, wondering why we didn't get Tank to be Santa. He's much more pleasant to deal with.

Badge places the plate on the mantle, ignoring the already stuffed stockings, and opens the bag. "I can't believe we have a fucking cactus and not a real tree," he says under his breath, but if I can hear him, the kids can too.

"For the love of all things vile, shut up!" I warn him, and Sarah pinches my butt. "Ow." I rub the tender spot. She lays her finger over her lips, telling me to shut up.

I'll show her how to shut up by stuffing my co—

"Get him!" Maizey warrior cries, and Aidan follows suit.

Everyone in the kitchen does their best to stay quiet when they hear the tiny squeals.

"You go right, I go left," Maizey orders.

"Oh no," I chuckle, watching as Maizey wraps a string of Christmas lights around Badge.

Aidan goes the other way, making sure Santa is stuck in the string of lights.

Maizey high kicks Badge in the belly, and he falls in a perfectly placed chair. Aidan wraps more lights around him and the chair, so Badge has nowhere to go. He's yelling at the top of his lungs, mouth open, chestnut colored hair glowing almost red against the Christmas lights. When he runs out of light, he does the only thing he knows to do with them.

Aidan plugs it in.

And Badge lights up in blues, oranges, yellows, reds, and greens. I see the annoyance in Santa's eyes, staring daggers right at me.

"We caught Santa!" Maizey squeals, and she and Aidan high five one another.

"Mommy, Daddy!" Maizey calls out for us, and Sarah intertwines her fingers with mine.

"I think that's our cue," Sarah says.

"Do we unwrap, Badge?" Skirt asks, peeking over my shoulder.

A RUTHLESS CHRISTMAS

"Nah, leave him like that for a while. It will be good for him," I say.

"This is the best Christmas ever," Warden says with a big smile on his face. Everyone gives him a hard glare, and he backtracks. "I don't mean the bad shit. I just mean now."

Bane throws his arm around his twin's shoulder. "I know what you meant."

"Mommy! I caught Santa. I caught Santa. Hurry, come see before he poofs away!" Maizey says with urgency.

Maybe Warden is right, maybe this is, right now, the best Christmas ever.

"We're going to take pictures of Badge like this, right? Blackmail him for the rest of time?" Poodle asks.

"Oh yeah, definitely."

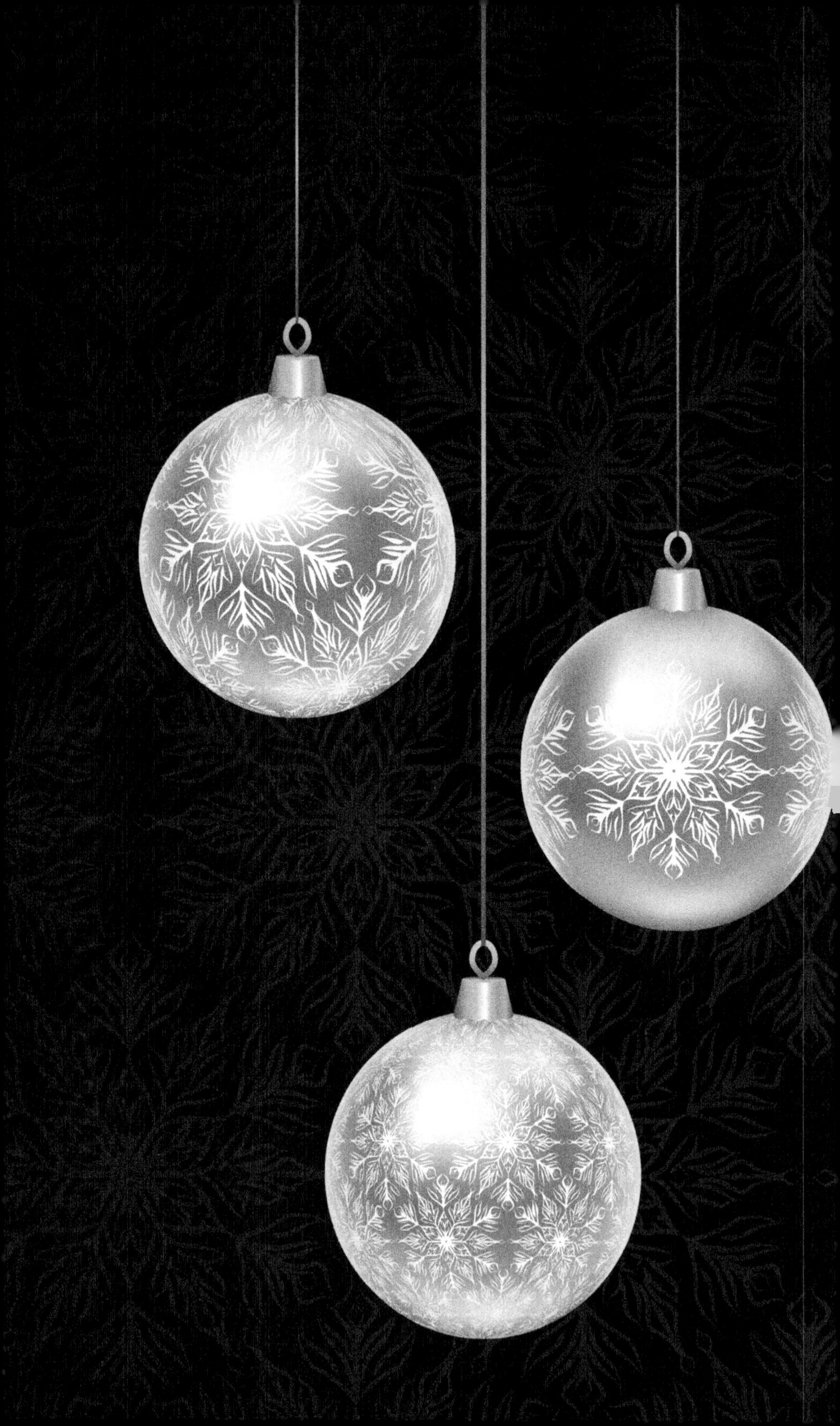

CHAPTER NINETEEN

Sarah

Christmas Day

"**C**AN YOU UNTIE ME NOW?" BADGE ASKS, WIGGLING AROUND in his chair. Aidan and Maizey crashed and fell asleep around his chair a few hours ago, but now it's about time to wake them up for presents. "I really need to take a piss."

"Badge, Santa does not say those words," I chuckle, then smell the sweet scent of coffee. "Yeah, I'll untie you." I unplug him and unwrap one string, going in a hundred circles before starting on the other.

"Good thing I'm not Santa. Ever again." Once he's free, he runs toward his room to get undressed and do his business. My cheeks still hurt from laughing at what the kids did. Scrubbing my eyes, I yawn and step over Aidan, who has his hand on top of Maizey's. Oh my God, what if they grow up and fall in love?

A mother can hope.

I throw my hair up in a quick, messy bun and head to the kitchen. Reaper, Patrick, Poodle, Warden, Bane, Wolf, and Boomer are there making Christmas breakfast.

"Is everyone ready for presents? The cactus is overflowing. Santa really outdid himself," I say, greeted by Reaper's kiss.

"Eat first, then we will."

"Aye, the kids will sleep for another half hour. Let's dig in before the little spawns wake up," Skirt says, biting into a piece of bacon.

Delilah comes up the steps of the basement next, holding the hands of the two kids we haven't seen much since we rescued them. Micah and Delaney, brothers.

Everyone stops what they're doing, looking up as they enter the kitchen, and the siblings hide behind Delilah's legs.

"Well, good morning, you two! Guess what? It's Christmas! Do you want to go open your gifts?" I ask them, wanting them to feel like part of the family.

Micah blinks at me and steps away from Delilah. "We have gifts?"

My heart breaks when I hear those words. "Of course, you do! Santa brings presents to everyone. Come on, everyone. Looks like we're moving to the living room early. Grab your coffee," I say, guiding the kids to the living room.

When they see the cactus, they're astounded. "Woah, that's the coolest tree ever."

"It's a cactus," Delaney says. "Stupid."

"You're stupid!" Micah pushes his brother, and he pushes back.

A RUTHLESS CHRISTMAS

"Okay, that's enough. Everyone, calm down. You're both right. It's a Christmas cactus," I say with pride.

"Maizey," Micah pokes her side. "Wake up. Christmas is here."

"We caught Santa!" She bolts into a sitting position, but then she sees the empty chair. "But he was right there! We caught him."

"He poofed. I saw it," I say, wanting her to know I believe her.

A knock at the door interrupts everyone getting settled, but Tank gets up as soon as he sits down. "I got it."

He opens the door, and Zain is there, holding a bottle of wine with a bow on it. "I … uh … I don't know if I'm still wanted here, but I wanted to bring something by. I didn't know what to get."

"I'm sorry, we don't allow alcohol in the main room," I tell him.

"Oh, it's non-alcoholic. I saw what Porter did to your friend," Zain says, and to know he was so thoughtful has Tank swinging the door open for him to come in.

"Come on in," I invite him in, and he gives me the biggest smile, one that is remarkably similar to Reaper's.

Reaper comes in the room and gives Zain a nod, which is better than a knife to the chest, so hopefully he understands that.

Everyone gets settled in the main room, and I can't help but feel overwhelmed with love. This is my family, my home, my people. There are so many here, so many who would risk their lives for another. I'm so lucky.

Poodle and Melissa are on the couch, feeding Lady

pancakes. They have given her everything she wasn't allowed to have before since she isn't doing so well. Patrick and Sunnie are next to them, Tool and Juliette are sitting next to Reaper on the floor to be close to the action. Doc and Joanna are on the other side of the cactus, Skirt and Dawn are on the loveseat, Joey on Skirt's lap. Aidan is in front of the tree, looking like he's about to tear into the gifts any minute now.

Tongue and Daphne are in the corner, watching from the dark as they like to do. Badge, Slingshot, Knives, Tank, Bullseye, and Braveheart are on the new sectional we just purchased. It's huge, an L-shape, to fit everyone.

That doesn't even include Boomer and his guys, who are lined up against the wall since there's no room.

Maybe we should have had Christmas in the gym...

"Okay, here we go," Reaper says, grabbing the first gift. "Slingshot, it's you, buddy," Reaper tosses it to him, and Slingshot catches the red gift with a silver bow.

He tears into it, opens the box, and jumps up and down when he sees what it is. "It's a three-hundred-dollar gift card to my favorite taco stand!"

No one is happy about it.

"Who did that?" Reaper asks, but no admits a thing.

"Duh, Daddy. Santa." Maizey pats Reaper's arm. "It's okay. It only means Slingshot deserved it."

"I'll have to write a letter to Santa and tell him my complaints then." Reaper shoots me a glance and winks, and my body flushes in response. He knows it too because his eyes darken to molten lava.

"Thanks, Santa!" Slingshot nudges Badge, and Badge slaps him on the back of the head.

A RUTHLESS CHRISTMAS

"Bullseye!" Reaper throws him a gift, and we hope it lightens Bullseye's spirit. He's been quiet and down. We miss him.

Bullseye tears into the black wrapping paper and grins, smiling for the first time in months. "A dart maker. I love it! Thank you, Reap—Santa," he corrects himself quickly. "Really, thank you."

"Daphne, this one is from Tongue. You have two," Reaper says, and Daphne manages to pry herself away from Tongue's hold to take the boxes.

One is wrapped in pink, and the other is wrapped in green. She gently unfolds each side of the paper instead of tearing into it. The box is long; maybe a necklace? No. That's too basic for Tongue.

"I love it!" she announces, sliding out a blade that looks a lot like Tongue's, but when the light hits it, I notice it has his name engraved in the steel. Not his road name, his real one.

"I got mine engraved too, Comet," Tongue says, unsheathing his knife to show her. "It's got your name on it."

Daphne kisses him, deep and long, and the guys whistle at them for putting on a show. She pulls away, flushed, and her eyes are glittering with lust. Tongue growls, and Reaper has to snap his fingers to get the couple to focus.

"What's this?" Daphne holds up a key, analyzing it by twisting the ribbon which causes it to spin in circles.

"It's the key to your new bookstore," Tongue says, kissing her on the cheek.

This time, there is no stopping them. Daphne jumps on Tongue, wraps her legs around him, and his hands move to her ass. I move my palm in front of Maizey's eyes, and Reaper does the same with Aidan. A few of Boomer's men take note and go to hide Micah and Delaney's eyes when Tongue walks backward to their room.

"I love it. I love you," Daphne says between kisses. "I want you so much."

"Okay, kids in the house. Kids!" Reaper calls after them just as their door slams. "Bunch of rowdy teenagers." Reaper shakes his head and gets up to grab the big box against the far wall.

"Boomer, here." Reaper hands him a box that isn't wrapped. "Sorry, I ran out of paper."

Boomer gives Reaper a bepuzzled look and yanks the box open. "Fireworks!" he gasps, then giggles. "Big ones. Holy crap, Reaper, Sarah, thank you. Can I go shoot one off now?"

"It isn't nighttime, Boomer," I deadpan.

"So…" he murmurs.

Everyone laughs, and Reaper continues handing out gifts until there is only one left. Even Boomer's men have a little something, cash to gift cards; something simple since we don't know them too well. Zain even has one, a small album full of pictures of Reaper and everyone here throughout the years so Zain can feel like part of the family. Tool has a new screwdriver set from Juliette, and Juliette has a new microphone, and Reaper and I got them new sex toys.

Skirt, Dawn, and Bullseye got a new room for their escapades. A real watch room. There's a private section where Bullseye can watch without Skirt and Dawn knowing, or he can join. We do know Skirt doesn't allow Bullseye to touch, but we wanted them to have a nicer room to share their desires besides the rooms the cut-sluts were in.

A RUTHLESS CHRISTMAS

Gross.

Reaper hands me a gift next. "I thought we agreed we wouldn't buy each other anything? I took that literally. I didn't get you a present."

"It's for both of us," he says.

"Okay." I lift a brow and pucker my lips as I carefully open the envelope. I pull out two plane tickets and a brochure. "Oh my God." I read the itinerary. "A week's vacation in Alaska! You're serious? How … when? You need to be here?"

"Tool can handle it. Maizey is going to hang out with Dawn and Skirt. Everything will be fine. Tool is VP for a reason. I want time with my wife. Me and you, Doll. Do you want that?"

Pinpricks sting my eyes as I try not to cry, but it's a losing battle. "Are you kidding? I'll go anywhere with you." This time, it's my turn to kiss him senseless. I can understand why Daphne took Tongue to the bedroom. I'm ready to tear his pants off and mount him standing.

"I have a gift for you two," Doc says, handing us a small package.

"You're under the mistletoe!" Maizey points to Knives and Mary.

They're arguing because Mary got him coal for Christmas, and he got her a pegged leg. A fake one, but she's currently beating him upside the head with it.

"I'd rather kiss a freaking toad then kiss Knives!" Mary slams the leg down on Knives' shoulder.

Knives wraps an arm around her waist and tugs her head back by her hair. "If it gets you to shut up, I'm willing to do anything!" He smashes his lips against her, and I'm nearly bursting at the seems with excitement. Finally.

They act like they hate each other, but they don't.

The kiss turns from angry to soft, and Mary pulls back, trying to blink away her daze. She shoves the wooden leg into Knives' stomach and stomps away.

"That woman is crazy!" Knives groans.

"Anyway," Doc clears his throat and offers us the gift again. It's cute, wrapped in a metallic green paper with a red satin bow. "You have to open it together."

Reaper and I tug the ends of each side of the bow, and the ribbon floats to the ground. We tear the paper off to reveal a piece of plastic. I'm staring at a positive sign right in the middle. "What is it?" I ask him. "Is it a life alert for Reaper?" I chuckle at my own joke, and everyone laughs with me.

I can be funny.

"Maybe. In about nine months. You're pregnant, Sarah. I re-ran the test. It's positive."

"It's—" I gasp, my words failing me. "It's p-p-pos… positive?" I whisper, and my hand trembles. "Really?" My voice becomes high-pitched as I cry.

"Really, Sarah. Merry Christmas," Doc grins.

Reaper and I stare at one another, not believing what we're seeing. Reaper falls to his knees in front of everyone and kisses my stomach. "Thank you, thank you, thank you," he chants.

"We're pregnant."

Reaper wraps his arms around me and lays his cheek against my stomach. "I love you."

A RUTHLESS CHRISTMAS

"I love you too." I run my hands through his hair, and he jumps to his feet. I stand back, stunned by the sudden movement.

He takes my hand and lifts it in the air. "We're pregnant!" he announces to everyone, and the entire MC cheers and claps.

It really is the best Christmas ever.

Because only the best miracles happen on Christmas.

A RUTHLESS CHRISTMAS PLAYLIST

HAPPY HOLIDAYS, YOU BASTARD BY BLINK-182

SANTA STOLE MY GIRLFRIEND BY THE MAINE

FOOL'S HOLIDAY BY ALL TIME LOW

MERRY CHRISTMAS, KISS MY ASS BY ALL TIME LOW

DON'T SHOOT ME SANTA BY THE KILLERS

DASHER BY GERARD WAY

YULE SHOOT YOUR EYE OUT BY FALL OUT BOY

GRANDMA GOT RUN OVER BY A REINDEER BY REEL BIG FISH

THIS CHRISTMAS (I'LL BURN IT TO THE GROUND) BY SET IT OFF

CHRISTMAS DRAG BY I DON'T KNOW HOW BUT THEY FOUND ME

ACKNOWLEDGMENTS

To my greedy Ruthless Readers thank you for being so supportive and helping us have a great first year.

To Give Me Books we owe you so much this year, you have been so supportive and helpful. Thanks for all you do.

To Wander and Andrey as always thanks for being our rock, words will never express just how much you mean to us.

Donna thanks for all you do, you are everything, my voice of reason, my ear when I need to vent, our biggest supporter and for that I'm so grateful. #BOOMERISDONNAS

To all the bloggers and reviewers, we appreciate the hell out of you, thanks for sticking by us.

Lynn thanks for being my other half and knowing when I need you before I do.

To the Instigator you make this possible, love you.

Harloe thanks for being you.

Silla thanks for all you do.

Stacey thanks for your amazing formatting.

Austin thanks for always being there and pushing me to be the best.

Mom thanks for believing in me.

Jeff FIVE LITTLE WORDS

ALSO BY K.L. SAVAGE

PREQUEL - REAPER'S RISE
BOOK ONE - REAPER
BOOK TWO - BOOMER
BOOK THREE - TOOL
BOOK FOUR - POODLE
BOOK FIVE - SKIRT
BOOK SIX - PIRATE
BOOK SEVEN - DOC
BOOK EIGHT - TONGUE
BOOK NINE – A RUTHLESS CHRISTMAS

OTHER BOOKS IN THE RUTHLESS KINGS SERIES
A RUTHLESS HALLOWEEN

RUTHLESS KINGS MC IS NOW ON AUDIBLE.

CLICK HERE TO JOIN RUTHLESS READERS AND GET THE LATEST UPDATES BEFORE ANYONE ELSE. OR VISIT AUTHORKLSAVAGE.COM OR STALK THEM AT THE SITES BELOW.

FACEBOOK | INSTAGRAM | RUTHLESS READERS
AMAZON | TWITTER | BOOKBUB | GOODREADS |
PINTEREST | WEBSITE

FOR UPDATES FROM K.L. SAVAGE TEXT:

KL SAVAGE

RUTHLESS ROMANCE THAT WILL *RIP* YOUR HEART OUT.

725-225-0825

Printed in Great Britain
by Amazon